BLOOD BOUND

Book 1 in the Bound Series

Hannah Crawford

HANNAH CRAWFORD

DEDICATION

May all of those who told you that you were never good enough, choke on it.

CHAPTER ONE

Arabella

I leaned against the cool glass; my arms splayed out with palms pressed on the banister as I looked down on those beneath me. Once an old gothic style catholic church, the place had been completely transformed into a nightclub. Black velvet surrounded me on every side, the red and purple lights pulsating to a William Control song reflecting off its shiny material. Several of the old pews had been converted into VIP booths behind me and on the lower floor were a few scattered metal cages, people in various forms of undress dancing in them seductively.

A strange scent of leather, cigarettes, and alcohol thickened the air but the energy, the depravity is what nearly took my breath away. I watched as the majority of them gravitated toward the marble dance floor, groping and grinding, their desperate need to be touched, to be used, on full display. But as I searched the crowded room, it wasn't a desire to be fucked by a stranger that brought me here.

The music transitioned into something faster, the bass vibrating beneath my shoes as I descended down the stairs. My anxiety was clawing away at my insides, the trainwreck in my brain forcing my hands to fidget wildly. Every fiber inside of me had been screaming danger since the moment I had arrived. It didn't help that I could feel their eyes on me, their desire to devour me wrapping around me like it wanted to suffocate me.

From what little intel Alexander had given me, this place was a cesspool for Mercenaries and demons alike. Unlike the Necros, with whom you could smell a mile away, or even Mercenaries that were illuminated by their Aura, Fiends were harder to identify. For the most part, they looked human unless you knew what you were looking for. And you could always tell by their eyes. The soullessness behind them was enough to make a person go insane if you stare into them long enough. And holy fuck could I feel them staring right now.

But I ignored their gazes, eluded their lustful touches as I pushed past the crowd of people, or rather a mix of people and those vile beings, and moved to the bar. I fucking hated crowded places and of course this had to be the first place I had to visit when I came back to this dreadful fucking city.

Hallowed Haven had always been crawling with the decaying breath of the Necros which is why it was home to 5 of the First families. Our job was to protect humans from the things they warn about in fairy tales and in exchange we get to live among them. As if that were actually a privilege. Most of them didn't even know of our existence and were blissfully unaware that they were grinding against the very things that would kill them. In fact, I was positive that some of them were fucking right there in front of everyone, sadistic desperate moans occasionally spilling out over the music. It was nauseating. And unfortunately, there seems to have been a huge influx of Fiends lately. What was once a strange phenomenon of a Demon showing signs of being consciously aware, was now a nightclub filled to the brim with the things we were born to kill.

I couldn't even last a solid 10 minutes before I felt like I wanted to rip my own skin off. With a sigh, I forced my way back through the debauchery and went outside. I desperately needed some fresh air to clear my running thoughts but as the cool night breeze hit my face, my phone sounded. I let it ring a few times before I finally answered.

"What the hell do you want?"

"Hello to you too," Alexander replied, irritation ripe in his tone.

"Can I help you with something?"

"Yes actually," he snapped. "What is taking you so long to give me an update?" His words came out in a hurry.

"Calm the fuck down," I exclaimed. "This is going to take some time. If it does exist, do you really think it would be that easy to find?"

"You better bite that tongue of yours. I'm not in the mood for your fucking attitude."

"Should have thought about that before you Bound me."

"A decision I still question if I regret." I only laughed in response. "Tell me, Arabella," he continued, his voice cruel. "What are you going to do if you run into one of them? If you must fight someone you know? If you had to kill one of them?" This time, I snapped back.

"Every one of them are dead to me."

"So feisty, Miss Blackwood," he laughed.

"Fuck you."

"Mmm, are you offering?" I snorted, refusing to give him the reaction he wanted.

"Not in a million years, Alexander... I'll bring you your stupid amulet when I fucking find it." With that, I hung up and failed to not stew on his words. It wasn't lost on me that I could run into someone that I knew and there was a strong possibility that one of them could have the Cursed Amulet. Or at least knew something about it.

The thought of being back in this town after 5 years was a huge source of the anxiety that's been crippling my ability to do my job since I got here. I've done some really sketchy things for Alexander in the last 5 years, things that still give me nightmares, to work off the debt that I owe him. Most of the time I can push it down, block off the part of my brain that gives a shit so that I can get the job done. An unhealthy coping mechanism, I know, but it's the only way I know how to get through it. So, I've been trying to convince myself that this was the same. Returning to the home, to the people that I ran away from and ended up under Alexander's thumb in the first place. Yeah, I know, I'm a fucking idiot.

With a few more forced deep breaths, I was going to make myself go back inside but then I felt it; that familiar burn instantly shooting through my veins. I walked toward the alleyway around the back of the place and that's where I found the three of them; two males and a female. The illuminated white Aura around her mixed with the intricate counterclockwise rune engraved on her upper arm, told me that not only was she a Mercenary but she was also a member of the Spiral. The rotten scent of ground up belladonna petals and the dried blood that coated the hazelwood dagger in one of their hands filled my nose. It was a concoction that was fatal to Mercenaries. So, these two were Hunters.

One held her down as the other held the blade to her neck, its coarse jagged edges scraping her skin. As strange as it was, this was what had caused that burning in me; one of my abilities as a Mercenary born from one of the First Families was my ability to sense when someone close by was going to die. To describe it, it was like taking a huge whiff of rubbing alcohol and it burns your nose. Except that burning instead spread through my entire body.

"Stop!" The male who held the knife turned to look at me

though neither released their grip on the girl.

"Leave," he said, his voice raspy and harsh. "This is none of your business."

"Oh, but it is," I replied, a cruel smile creeping across my face. "Let her go." Both of them laughed.

"And what will you do? Stop me?" He looked me up and down, clearly unintimidated by my presence. Good; I liked when I took them by surprise, and I could really go for a fight to release some of this pent-up turmoil in me. Finally, the one without the knife let go of the girl and stepped toward me.

"I'd stop while you're ahead." Another step.

"You are a pretty one," he laughed. "Once I'm through with her, maybe I'll show you why you should mind your own business." As he said it, I watched him grab his dick and lick his dry, cracked lips as he undoubtedly pictured what he was going to do to me. I made a gagging motion as the thought filled me with repulsion.

As he took his last step, I lifted my right hand as if to wave him off. I watched with twisted excitement as his chest buckled over his knees, his body turning and his bones snapping in loud succession. He dropped to the ground, his body convulsing while he screamed in agony. As he watched his perverted friend die, the other man let go of the girl, pushing her hard onto the ground before running toward me.

"Run!" I shouted toward her and without hesitation, she took off. I allowed him to grab me, his hands gripping the hair at the nape of my neck.

"How did you do that?" he said through clenched teeth. "You didn't even touch him!" I smiled, which pissed him off even more and his grip tightened. I wanted to yell out in pain, but I bit my tongue and replied calmly.

"I don't have to." In that moment I watched the fear well

up in his eyes and he made a split decision to try and slam the dagger into my chest. I brought my hand up just in time, the blade slamming into my palm before he ripped it back out. I cried out as I felt the poison sear through my flesh, but I couldn't let him take me off guard. Using my other hand, I reached up and grabbed his cheek, sending a quick pulse through him. Finally, he let go of my hair as blood started to seep from his every orifice and panic painted his face.

"You fucking bitch!" he screamed. "What did you do to me?" A wicked grin spread from ear to ear as I reached out and grabbed him again, this time filling his veins like a poison.

"Exactly what you fucking deserve." He dropped to the ground, still clawing at his face and arms as it spread through him like a virus until he was nothing more than a bloody pile of filth.

"Holy Shit!" I jumped at the sound of her voice. "How the hell did you do that?"

"I told you to run," I sighed, walking over to pick up the dagger. I started back toward the front of the building, desperate to get out of there before I was seen. Not to mention the smell of fresh blood was bound to draw the attention of whatever Necro may have been close by and I wasn't fully equipped for that kind of fight right now. Plus, my hand was starting to burn.

"Wait!" She called, following close behind me. "Are you also a member of The Spiral?"

"Fuck no," I exclaimed and snapped back around to face her. "Stop following me." That was when I realized how young she really was. She reminded me of a baby doll; soft tawny skin, rosy cheeks, chocolate brown eyes and chest length brunette hair pulled back in pigtails. I guess the Spiral was getting so desperate for obedient followers that they resorted to accepting children. "What are you doing here anyways?"

"They brought me here," she said, her voice small,

terrified. "I was working on an assignment for the Spiral... that's all I remember." I shook my head.

"That was your first mistake. Jeez, how old are you? 14?"

"I just turned 18 actually," she replied. I rolled my eyes.

"Oh, forgive me," I replied sarcastically. "Here I thought you were still a child." She protested, sticking her tongue out and making a pouting noise, further proving my point. I turned away from her again, continuing toward my old black Honda Accord that has gotten me out of some sticky situations on more than one occasion. There was even still a crack in the windshield from the time I hit a demon with my car. I threw the door open, tossing the dagger onto the passenger side floor. Gods, my hand was fucking aching.

"You need to get that checked out," she said. "I can take you to my brother. My adopted brother, anyway."

"No," I snapped. "I'm fine."

"Jeez, you're so grouchy," she laughed.

"No, I just don't need any help. Do you have a way to get back to somewhere safe?"

"My brother owns this place." She motioned toward the club. It wasn't unusual for a Mercenary to have multiple forms of income. Fighting Demons didn't pay quite as much as one would think and although the First Families came from old money, they had to make sure that money never ran out. So it didn't surprise me that a powerful Mercenary owned this place. But it was strange that they allowed it to be overrun with those gross fucking creatures that held no qualms for fucking each other, even sometimes their prey, right there in front of others. "I'll just have him take me home."

"Fine," I replied as I got in my car. "Then go find him." I started the ignition and tried to close the door, but she stopped me again.

"Wait!"

"What do you want?"

"What's your name?"

"If I tell you, will you go away?" She nodded, a smile lifting her lips. "Bella." She gave me an eerie smile and it irritated me. "What?" She shook her, refusing to answer. "You really know how to test someone's patience! Leave me alone."

"It's not him, you know."

"What?"

"He doesn't have what you are looking for."

I sighed, frustrated, "Who said I was looking for anything?"

"The Cursed amulet is here. But you won't find it in him." That stopped me dead in my tracks. "Goodbye, Bella. I will see you again soon." With that, she skipped away, and I never thought I would regret saving someone's life...

CHAPTER TWO

That night, I didn't sleep well. It wasn't really the fact that my hand hurt so bad I seriously contemplated cutting it off. It wasn't even what she had said to me. It was the fact that every time I closed my eyes, I saw Damian; his hands around my throat, the look in his eyes when he was about to kill me. I knew that being back in this town was going to drudge up memories. But it was all the memories that I desperately claimed no longer mattered to me.

When it was a decent time to be awake on a Saturday morning, I headed for the kitchen. Alexander had insisted that I stayed with a contact of his while I was here so he could keep a better eye on me. Instead, I stayed in a hotel room, on Alexander's dime, just to piss him off because that was the one thing I was good at. I made sure it even had a fully equipped kitchen but not so that I'd be able to properly handle my nutrition. But because I wanted to be able to have a decent cup of coffee in the morning. And this morning, I drank it black, not even bothering to add any flavor. I just needed the caffeine.

After my second cup, I tried, unsuccessfully, to stop my hand from aching. Normally I could use my Aura to heal, though healing had never been my strong suit. However, because of the poison, I couldn't. As I had said before, one of the only ways to stop a Mercenary was belladonna and dead blood. Sure, we could die by other means, but it was a lot harder to do so. Our bodies were meant to handle fighting demons but if you wanted to render one of us almost useless, belladonna and dried blood was the way to go. It acted like a numbing agent, dulling our abilities enough for someone to take us out. If your Aura was considered weak by any means, it could kill you. A stab in the hand was no reason to start confessing my biggest regrets on my deathbed. But man, it hurt like hell!

Eventually, I gave up and tried to ignore the pain by getting ready for the day. I jumped in the shower before throwing on a pair of black jeans and a matching hoodie. I even threw on a little makeup to hide the dark circles under my eyes. I cleaned my hand up one last time before wrapping it tightly, hoping the pressure would ease some of the pain.

My phone had been off the entire morning, so I wasn't exactly surprised when I was flooded with messages and missed calls. With a sigh, I braced myself for his yelling before I called him back. He answered on the first ring. Yeah, he was pissed.

"I swear to the Gods you will be the fucking death of me!" He yelled so loud I had to pull the phone away from my ear. I couldn't help but laugh. "Is something funny to you?"

"Not at all," I replied, my tone dripping in mockery.

"Damn it, Arabella I thought something had happened to you," he retorted.

"Aw such a caring boss. I told you not to worry about me. This is no different than any other job I've done for you. I can handle myself. I don't need you checking up on me every five minutes."

"Really? Is that why you were almost killed by two hunters last night?

"How did you know about that?"

"Did you really think I'd let you go out there without having anyone else keeping an eye on you? I am many things, but stupid is not one of them."

"I took care of them."

"What about the girl?"

"She's innocent, Alexander." He let out a frustrated sigh.

"Why can't you just listen to me?"

"Because I'm not a child. Are you forgetting that I managed to steal from you?" He didn't say anything, but I could picture the frustration on his face. "Let me do my job so I can break this bind once and for all and then you can be done with me."

When I had agreed to come back to Hallowed Haven, having been promised that this job would be enough to pay off my remaining debt to Alexander, the thought of running into someone that I knew was on the back burner of my mind. Not completely gone. As I said, it was a huge source of anxiety. But I kept it at the bottom of the list of things I had to deal with right now, you know shoved it down into that place to make me forget. But on my way to meet up with 2 of Alexander's contacts, the thought was making my skin crawl. As I walked, I kept my hood up and my head down, although I think it just drew more attention than I wanted.

I lost all contact with anyone that had anything to do with this place, including the rest of the Blackwood family. And that wasn't an easy task. Along with the other First families that co-inhabit this city, the Blackwood family was powerful and dangerous. Malachi Blackwood liked things in order and to go his way which is why he wouldn't take too kindly to his own daughter running off and disappearing. So, a family reunion wasn't a part of my plan, and I was going to avoid it at all costs. But as I walked, I felt like everyone I passed stared just a little too long; paid a little too much attention to me. I was just short of paranoia by the time I made it to my destination.

I walked toward the back of a very shady looking apartment building, to a half empty parking garage. I swear if he was taking me out here to kill me... I found two people waiting. One was a male with smooth umbre skin and was huge, at least a foot and a half taller than my 5'3 self and had more muscle than should be legal. He reminded me of someone who had been in the military as he stood with his hands behind his back and his hair was buzzed, even donned a dark green t-shirt with camo cargo pants that looked like they were too tight.

The second was a female with bronze skin that screamed of a hard life. She was just an inch or so taller than me and her long dark hair was braided at her back. She was fit with a deadpan stare that could kill and despite the apathetic approach, she was clad in a pink camo outfit similar to Mr. Muscles. Both were unwavering as I approached them but the sight of them kind of made me want to giggle.

"Hello Miss Blackwood," the man said, his voice a deep baritone.

"Hello," I replied. "Alexander isn't kidding about his privacy, is he?" I was trying to lighten the tension but of course it didn't work. The woman had a Brazilian accent, and her voice was devout of any emotion as she replied.

"Alexander has left a list of names. He believes that one of them could have information about the Amulet. He wants you to investigate all of them and retrieve whatever information you can." She pulled the piece of paper from her back pocket and handed it to me. "Kill them if you have to. He also wants you to keep Taylor and I informed on everything that may be helpful information."

"Oh, I'll be sure to do just that," I replied with an amused smile.

"Something funny?" I only smiled and started to walk

away.

"Miss Blackwood," Taylor called after me.

"Yes?" I replied sweetly over my shoulder.

"We will be watching you." This time I laughed out loud but said nothing more as I left the parking garage. I probably should have just gone back to the hotel so I could create a game plan. But I felt a groan in my stomach and realized that I haven't eaten in way longer than I wanted to admit. Just down the road from my hotel was a diner that I vaguely remembered from a distant childhood memory, and the strong smell of French fries and coffee really pulled me as my stomach growled in approval.

I slipped into the building and sat at a small booth at the back of the joint before pulling the list from my jacket pocket. I placed it down on the table as the waiter walked up. I ordered coffee and a plate of fries before sending him away again. I skimmed over the list.

Alexei Sokolov.

The Spider.

Keiran Stark.

My heart dropped. The Starks were a family I wanted to avoid more than my own, after Damian Stark tried to kill me. Keiran Stark was his younger brother. He was also, at one point, my best friend.

"Bella!" The sound of her voice made me jump and I looked up to see the girl from last night bouncing toward me. She wasn't alone, though the man with her had walked up to the front of the diner, capturing the attention of the blond behind the counter.

"You don't go away, do you?" She smiled as she shook her head, her face giddy.

"I'm Emery by the way." I only nodded. "How is your

hand?"

"Hurts like hell."

"My brother can help with that. He's just over there." She pointed at the guy flirting with the blond who had his back towards us.

"I told you, I'm fine. I don't need your help."

"You are so stubborn, Arabella." My head snapped up to look at her.

"How do you know that name?"

"That is a name that everyone still talks about. Especially my brother."

"And why is that?"

"Because Keiran has been looking for you for quite some time, silly." She said it like it was supposed to make all the fucking sense in the world to me. I froze.

"The Starks don't have a sister," I replied, my voice feeling small.

"I told you, I'm sort of adopted."

"Great story, but I think you have me mixed up with someone else." I stood up, feeling more nauseated than hungry at this point, and shoved the list back into my pocket.

"Where are you going?"

"I- I need to go." I went for the door, trying to slip out before he turned around and saw me. I was almost there before someone grabbed my arm. "Look, Em-" My mouth slammed shut.

He was different. Though he was only 28, he seemed so much older but in a fine wine kind of way. His hair was now his natural black, no longer the blood red color that he used to have when we were younger, and it was longer, reaching just below his ears as several strands fell into his handsome, stoic face. He was just a couple shades darker than what one would consider pale, and it made those gray blue eyes I had once been so fond of look even more sultry. He was about a foot taller than me and the tight black clothing he wore clung to his muscles like they were going to escape. He was intimidating, and I found it hard to look at him as I dropped my eyes to the ground. Oh shit.

"What are you doing here?" His voice was harsh. "Answer me damn it."

"Keiran stop," Emery said from behind him, her face annoyed.

"Is this why you brought me here?" He turned his aggression toward her. "Why you were so fucking persistent on driving across town for this place! She's not someone you should be involved with!" I pulled away from him, breaking the vice grip he had around my arm.

"She saved my life!" She exclaimed in frustration.

"What are you talking about?"

"Two of his hunters almost killed me last night!" His hunters? "She almost died trying to help me and you are being an asshole!" Her tone was exasperated as if she had explained this once before. He turned his gaze back to me and I felt like I was stuck underneath a heat lamp, its light burning a fucking hole through me.

"She never does anything without selfish reasons," he replied, his voice distasteful.

"Fuck off, Keiran," I snapped.

"So, she does speak."

"I saved her because she's one of us. And fuck you for saying otherwise." I turned away from them again, my hand on the door handle.

"Wait." He reached for me, but I recoiled from his touch.

"Don't fucking touch me!" I stormed out of the diner, ignoring Emery's call for me to come back.

I practically ran back to the hotel and once I was safely hidden behind its walls, I crashed out. Of everyone in this fucking town, it was Keiran that had to own the club? I never wanted to hear the name Stark again and now Emery seems determined for us to interact.

To be honest, I contemplated leaving. But if I did that, I would be proving Alexander right, that I couldn't handle this job. The last thing I wanted was for him to hold it above me and I really wanted to be rid of his fucking Bind. I swore that I had left everything that held me to this town behind, that it meant nothing. But the moment I saw him, all of my self-control went away. I dropped my head into my hands. Fuck was the only word running through my head... fuck, fuck, fuck!

I let my self-loathing take up most of the rest of my morning before I threw myself down on the bed around 10 am. I was exhausted, physically from last and now emotionally. I turned the tv on and flipped through the channels before I settled on watching Penny Dreadful reruns.

CHAPTER THREE

Keiran

"If you are hungry, Sakura said that she could have made you your breakfast," I said as I threw the car into park. Emery vigorously shook her head.

"No, it has to be here." She was excited as she jumped out of the car before I could protest further. I shook my head but with a laugh, I followed her inside the run-down building. I'm not sure why she chose here. Emery would eat the same exact thing for breakfast every morning. A bagel with butter, honey, and flaky sea salt with 2 eggs cooked sunny side up. It was like a morning routine that she had to follow, or she'd have an attitude for the rest of the day until she could go to sleep and start over again. But now she was dead set, since last night, on coming to this old diner on the other side of town.

She barreled through the door and headed toward the back booths as I made a quick note of how many people were inside. Besides the young couple who looked like they were nursing last night's hangover, another in the back with her hood up, trying unsuccessfully to hide the fact that she was there, and the staff, the place was nearly deserted.

The beautiful blond behind the counter looked up with

her warm brown eyes and blushed as I met her gaze. Maybe coming here would benefit me after all. She watched me intensely, biting seductively on her lower lip as I flashed her a grin and joined her at the counter.

"Good morning," she purred, her voice sweet.

"Good morning, beautiful," I replied equally as flirtatiously. She blushed and nervously played with the hem of her apron.

"What can I get for you?"

"I'm not too sure," I admitted. "Perhaps you can give me some suggestions." She furrowed her brow as if to think of what I might like.

"Well, the special today is a veggie omelet." I shrugged.

"Sounds like a safe choice. What's your favorite?"

"Well, I like-" I tried to pay attention to what she was saying as I heard Emery's voice behind me.

"Where are you going?" Emery asked.

"I- I need to go," a woman said as I turned from the waitress. I felt her push by me in a hurry and Emery was following close behind her, clearly upset. I grabbed the woman, pulling her back to see what the problem was.

"Look, Em-" She stopped speaking as those emerald green eyes met mine and for a moment, I wasn't sure I was really standing here. Five years. Five fucking years I had searched for Arabella Blackwood, longed to look into those green eyes again and beg for her forgiveness.

And fuck was she more beautiful than I remembered. Although she looked thin, her long black hair fell around her face, her porcelain skin flushed a bright shade of red and her full lips slightly parted as she dropped those hypnotic eyes away from me. I had thought about this very moment for five years, about what I would say but suddenly I realized I was wholly unprepared.

"What are you doing here?" My words came out in a rush and much angrier than I intended them to. "Answer me damn it!"

"Keiran stop," Emery snapped. I felt a wave of emotion as I realized why Emery had picked this diner. She had seen it in one of her visions. I wasn't angry because she brought me here, but a little fucking warning would have been nice.

"Is this why you brought me here? Why you were so fucking persistent on driving across town for this place! She's not someone you should be involved with!" Not only was I angry, but I was hurt. The things I had done to be able to find this woman were not for the weak. The things I still had to do. And yet here she stood in front of me thinking that she could hide behind the hood of a sweater. She pulled her arm away from me, the loss of contact making a ball form in my chest.

"She saved my life!" Emery yelled dramatically.

"What are you talking about?"

"Two of his hunters almost killed me last night! She almost died trying to help me and you are being an asshole!" Her tone was high pitched, as it usually was when she was acting like she was throwing a fit. My gaze found its way back to Arabella. There was a time when she would look at me like I was the only thing to bring her solace in this world. Now she was just squirming under my gaze.

"She never does anything without selfish reasons."

"Fuck off, Keiran," she snapped.

"So, she does speak." Oh, how I have missed that voice and that bratty attitude that turned me on more times than I should admit.

"I saved her because she's one of us." This time she met my

gaze defiantly. "And fuck you for saying otherwise." She turned away from me again, her hand reaching for the door handle.

"Wait." I reached for her, afraid that she was going to disappear again.

"Don't fucking touch me!"

"Arabella, wait!" Emery called out for her, but it was too late. I'm not sure how long I stood there. Maybe a minute, or ten, but it felt like an eternity as I watched her leave, unable to move. "You should go after her."

"Is everything okay?" The waitress's voice sounded faint, like background noise and it still took me a moment before I could turn back to her. Her brows were furrowed together, concern on her gentle face. I nodded.

"Forgive me, ma'am," I said, suddenly sounding more formal than before. "I don't think I'm hungry anymore." I watched the disappointment flood her face, but it disappeared just as quickly when her boss came barreling out of the back room.

"That girl didn't even pay for her order!" He was wiping his greasy hands on his dirty apron.

"I'll take care of it," I offered. "And keep the change for the inconvenience." I handed the middle-aged man a hundred-dollar bill and his dull brown eyes crinkled with a smile.

"Th-thank you sir," he said with excitement.

"Here's your receipt!" There was a pep in her step as the waitress handed me the small piece of paper. I went to place it in my pocket when I noticed her number written underneath the name Lacey and the words 'Call Me'. I only flashed her a grin before turning to leave.

"Let's go, Emery." She made a pouting noise but followed me back out to the car. "I need to go see someone."

CHAPTER FOUR

The old wooden floorboards groaned beneath my heavy boots as I stood in the living room. The place was stuffy, not that it ever had been refreshing to be in my family home. But seeing as I hadn't stepped foot in it since the night Arabella disappeared, the air was filled with dust and regret. A thick layer of dirt and filth lay over every inch of this place, from the white sheets covering the furniture to the dusty pictures that lined the old fireplace, and I thought it was a fitting depiction of how I felt at the moment. Heavy with forcefully forgotten memories and untouched by any semblance of love or care.

As if the place couldn't taunt me further, visual depictions of being here started playing in front me like an old movie. Running through the hallway, my mother close behind as her singsong voice echoed through the wood and the sounds of our laughter ricocheted off the walls. One of the few happy memories I had in this place that wasn't tainted with the receiving end of my father's aggression.

I had been meaning to get rid of this house and the painful memories it held. Specifically, the one where I watched Elisabeth die and she told me that if I ever ended up like my father, she'd come back and kill me herself. Where she begged me not to end up on the wrong side of the fight she swore was coming. I tried my best to do as she asked but I could almost hear my mother's voice telling me how much I truly fucked up. But she'd also tell me that this was the Gods' way of giving me a second chance and if I didn't take it, then I deserved whatever happened.

I released a sigh, my hand going to the back of my neck as I cracked it from side to side before I made way through the house. Without realizing that I was doing so, I ran my fingers along the way, leaving lines through the dust that coated them until I reached what used to be my room. I twisted the door handle, the cold metal biting into my palm, before pushing the door open with a little force to fight the old swollen wood. The room looked as if someone had left in a hurry; bed unmade and clothes still scattered across the floor. A grimy lamp that I probably never even shut off until the light bulb eventually burned out. I suppose I had; left in a hurry but I pushed the memory from my mind for now.

From my force to open the door, more dust had been thrown around. I coughed, accidentally inhaling some of it before covering my mouth and worked quickly to grab what it is that I came here for. Using my hand that wasn't covering my face, I managed to slide open the old desk drawer and retrieved the little black box from it and stuck it in the pocket of my jacket.

I paid no more mind to the feeling of dread that coated this place as I hurried back through, locking the old French doors behind me and joined Emery back at the car. She knit her eyebrows together in confusion as I threw the car into reverse, wanting more than I was letting on, to get the fuck out of here.

"I thought you had to go see someone?" she asked, her focus only half on me and the other half on the phone in her hand, a video playing of a new TikTok dance trend that I'm sure she was going to try and recreate with Sakura later.

"I do," I said. "I just needed to grab something first." This time she clicked her phone off, sliding it into the front pocket of her hoodie, before I felt her gaze boring into the side of my face. "What?"

"You shouldn't have let her just walk away," she said, her tone annoyed. I sighed.

"And you should have warned me about what I was walking into." I snuck a glance at her, her small features pinched together as if to say I'm the one with the misplaced audacity.

"Then you would have gone in there like you always do."

"What does that mean?" She sighed dramatically.

"You would have scared her off before you even had a chance to talk to her." She moved to sit cross legged in her seat, her hands resting on the sides of her face as if she were swooning over something. "She's like a scared little doe that you have to approach with caution."

"Arabella Blackwood is far from a scared little doe," I defended. "I watched her take down 2 Necros at one time and walked away without a scratch." And I remembered being seriously turned on by it when she looked at me with such pride after she did it... Fuck I really needed to get laid.

"Yeah, but that was a long time ago," she whined, her voice pulling me out of the inappropriate thought. "You don't know what she would have done if you came barreling toward her now." She looked away, a thought crossing her mind as she giggled. "Although, it would have been funny if you had, and she kicked your ass." I sat quietly for a moment, my thoughts running rampant.

"I probably would have let her," I admitted, my voice almost saddened. "It would have been a better reaction than the way she looked at me back at the diner." She puffed her cheeks out, blowing all the air from her lungs with a ridiculous sigh.

"You're going to have to forgive yourself at some point, Keiran," she said, her tone softer. I didn't say another word as we pulled up to the cemetery, and she stayed in the passenger seat with her hands folded in her lap, as I exited the car. "Tell your mom, I said hello." Her words hit me before I closed the door, and I threw her a quick smile before crossing to the other side. It was a short walk between the road and my mother's final resting place. Well, at least the headstone and memorial I had made for her ashes under an old willow tree that sat at the base of the embankment. She used to tell me that their branches held more secrets than we could fathom, that's why they drooped so low, holding the weight of the world in their limbs. This was why they were her favorite because she too knew what it was like to be weighed down by secrets...

I placed the wildflowers that I plucked along the way at the base of the marble headstone that read Elisabeth Stark and more unpleasant memories clouded my head.

I was fifteen when she died. For days after my mother's death, I was nothing more than a hollow shell, my hatred for the world that took her from me painted on my face like a warning sign. And I wanted someone else to feel just an ounce of that pain. I needed someone to blame.

I had planned to tell Arabella what my mother had said to me as she was dying, tell her that she was the reason that led us to this point, during my mother's funeral. I stood toward the back of the wake, my hands fisted together in anger as I mulled over in my head how I was going to tell everyone what she had said to me. I had been so preoccupied that I hadn't sensed her behind me until her tiny hand slid in mine. I turned and looked into her big green eyes, filled with just as much sadness as I felt, and I froze.

"What are you doing?" I asked. Arabella smiled, a genuine grin that even then melted my tough exterior.

"Reminding you that you aren't alone."

I shook my head, grinding the heel of my boot into the

compacted dirt beneath me as if to ground me back in the present. I pulled the box from my pocket, wiping the dust off as best as I could before I popped it open. Unlike the exterior, the inside of the box was perfectly clean, the small diamond encrusted ring shining on display in the middle. It wasn't anything fancy, and despite the hatred that my father had for my mother, she wore this wedding ring with pride. She had picked it out herself, with a matching one for my father that he never wore. As if he was the one that was embarrassed by her. As if she were blessed to have a marriage to such a despicable man. I scoffed, snapping the box shut and putting it back into my pocket.

"I promise I'm going to fix it, Elisabeth," I said, pinching the bridge of my nose. "And this time, I'm not going to let her slip through my fingers."

CHAPTER FIVE

Arabella

I hadn't realized I fell asleep until I woke up and it was dark in the room. I stretched and reached for my phone and saw that it was almost 9 o'clock at night. I had slept the entire day away and to my surprise, I wasn't bombarded with a slew of messages. Only one telling me that I was being given the space I needed to do my work but that he was still an impatient man and wanted me to message him as soon as I had anything worth sharing on the contents of the list.

While I had technically run into one of them, I wasn't about to tell him about it. I'm sure it would just make him question me again and I didn't have much argue left in me right now... I really was exhausted.

But I had somewhere to be, recon to do so, I texted him and told him that his 2 contacts this morning were lovely, and I could tell that the girl and I were going to be best friends. Maybe even go get our nails done together. He wasn't amused as he just said behave and be careful who I speak to. I rolled my eyes and tossed the phone back onto the bed.

I wasted way more time than I wanted on my little afternoon nap and decided to go back to the club, hoping to find anything at this point. Even though I now knew that Keiran owned the place, another detail that I probably should have shared with Alexander, I realized this was why so many of our kind hung out there and someone was bound to know something about the amulet. Though, it bothered me that he allowed the place to be tainted with Fiends. He always had a strict belief that a demon was a demon no matter what and they couldn't be forgiven for the things they had done. And now he allowed them to co-inhabit?

I suppose a lot could change in 5 years and I could speculate all I wanted to, but my best bet was to ask him directly, even if he was pissed that I was back. Plus, I knew nothing about this town any longer and as much as I hated the idea with a passion, I could use his help. If anything, Emery seemed more than willing to speak with me. I'd probably be able to get her to help.

I slipped out of my jeans and hoodie and rummaged through my clothes. I found a tight-fitting little black dress that would draw the attention of someone in power. Kieran had always been a flirt and though we never did anything other than kiss once when we were teenagers, the desire was always there. And I was hoping that it didn't completely burn away since the last time we saw each other so that I could use it to get his attention and make him talk. It was manipulative, I know, but it was the only avenue I had right now. I did up my long black hair in loose curls that fell down my back and did my makeup in a vintage pinup style with a gorgeous red lip. To finish the look, I grabbed my 6-inch black stilettos with the red bottoms though I had my doc martens at the ready in case I needed to get away quickly for any reason.

As I was walking through the door, I stopped for one last vanity look through the mirror. Puberty had hit me hard when I went from a scrawny child to having double ds and an ass that made it incredibly hard to find a decent pair of jeans that fit it and my waist. And though the dress accented my hourglass figure well, I could definitely tell that I had lost some weight as I looked myself over. Apart from that, the shoes made my legs look fantastic and it was one of the rare instances when I felt beautiful. I was certainly going to draw someone's attention. I just hoped it was the right someone.

****

It was busier tonight than the previous night, most likely due to it now being the weekend. I groaned. Not only were there more people to avoid, but my chances of one of those people being someone else that I knew, was a lot bigger. I also hadn't encountered a single Necro since being back which was starting to make me feel uneasy, so I kept my senses on extra high alert.

Most of the patrons flooded the dance floor again, their bodies twisting and swaying desperately to the music. There were few that lingered around the booths and both men and women scantily clad in leather danced on display in the metal cages. I managed my way through them, my sights set on the bartender.

"Can I have a White Russian please?" I asked sweetly as I took my place at a bar stool.

"Babe you can have whatever you like," he replied, an inviting and flirtatious smile on his face.

"Thank you," I giggled playfully. We held small talk for a few minutes before he set the drink down in front of me. I drank half of it in one sip, loving the cool feeling as it slid down my throat. He chuckled but was soon pulled away as two drunken males stumbled up across from us. As he stepped away, I let my eyes wander, searching for anything that would be of help to me.

"My, my Miss Blackwood, you are a sight for sore eyes." I turned and met that intimidating gray blue gaze. I rolled my eyes, hoping that the flashing lights were enough to hide my blush.

"I'd prefer to just make you go blind," I replied, trying to sound uninterested. He only smirked as he took the stool beside me, his gaze never leaving mine until I had to look away.

"What are you doing here, Arabella?" His tone was emotionless.

"I, Sir, am having a drink. Isn't that what people do at places like this?"

"Glad to see your sarcasm is still intact."

"And never better," I replied and raised my glass to him before taking a drink.

"You know what I meant." I saw his jaw clench and it frustrated the hell out of me that I found it attractive.

"What are you doing here, Keiran?" He grinned again.

"I own it."

"Then shouldn't you be getting back to work?" I took another drink, studying him.

"Actually-" He scooted closer to me "I think I'll stay right here with you." Before I could react, his hand was on my knee, inching higher up the side of my thigh. I scooted back but he was quicker than me and his grip on me tightened. "You wanted my attention. That's why you came here, right? Now you have it." His smile was wicked, and it made the muscles low in my belly clench. Though he was right, I pushed him away from me, the feel of his hands making me dizzy.

"You ruined the chance for that kind of attention the moment I found you fucking my sister, Keiran," I snapped. "I told you not to ever touch me again." I walked away from him, back toward the crowd of people that were oblivious to anything around them and went outside. I wasn't even sure if I was mad at him or mad that I fucking wanted it. It had been nearly a year since I had slept with a man and until that moment, it didn't bother me. I was perfectly capable of getting my rocks off on my own. But as soon as he touched me, it felt like an electric shock between my thighs. I had just reached the car when an arm was around my waist, spinning me around. Keiran pressed me against the cool door which made me shiver. "What the fuck?"

"Why did you come back, Arabella?"

"Let me go." He shook his head. "Damn it, Keiran. What does it matter to you?"

"Because I spent five fucking years looking for you. Then you show up like nothing fucking happened? I'm not buying that shit."

"You don't have to. I have my reason."

"Tell me what it is."

"Don't worry about it." I tried to wiggle out of his embrace, but his grip only tightened. It was like fighting a freaking bear.

"I will not let you go until you give me something." I bit down hard on my lip, growing increasingly tired trying to get out of his arms.

"I'm trying to find the Cursed Amulet," I cried. His arm loosened just a fraction.

"What?"

"I have to find it or else I will be in some serious shit."

"With who?" I shook my head.

"I can't tell you that."

"Why not?"

"Because I can't, Keiran." My voice was pleading at this point.

"Why here?"

"I don't know," I admitted. "This place has always been crawling with fucking Mercenaries; it wouldn't surprise me if one of the First families had it... can you please let me go?" Finally, his arm dropped away from me, and he stepped back, putting about a foot's distance between us.

"Have you found anything?"

"Now why would I share that information with you?"

"Because I can help you."

"This morning, I was selfish and now you want to help me?" He frowned.

"I didn't mean that."

"Yes, you did. You don't have to make me feel better."

"You disappeared without a trace, Arabella, and now here you are. There were so many emotions welling up inside of me the moment I saw you and I know that I should have handled it better. You were the last thing I was expecting when Emery said she wanted to go to the diner."

"Since when do you have a sister by the way?"

"Her family was killed by hunters. One night I found her rummaging through the trash behind the club, so I took her in." What a bleeding heart. "She is... a character." This time he chuckled. "She's also a seer. Which is why she knew you would be there."

"So that is why she knew what I was looking for." My tone was annoyed because already, too many people knew that I was here. I shook my head. "I don't need anyone getting in my way. You can just pretend that I'm not even here."

"You really expect me to do that? I've been looking for you since the moment you told me you never wanted to see me again."

"Because the image of my sister on top of you was etched

into my fucking brain!" Never mind the fact that the same night I found the two of them together was the night that his brother attacked me outside of the bar that I was desperately trying to drown my sorrows in. Unconsciously, I put my hand on my neck, remembering the heavy feeling of his hands around my throat. I shook my head, trying to suppress the memory. "Regardless, I'm not here to reminisce on old feelings. I'm here to do a job."

"And act like there was never any past between us?"

"If it means getting this job done quickly, then yes." He shook head.

"I can't act like you don't exist, Arabella. Like the unfinished business between us is just nonexistent." I pressed my lips, annoyed as I turned and got into the car.

"Then I will do it on my own." Before I could close the door, he stepped in front of it quickly and ducked down to meet my gaze. The intensity in his stare made me want to look away again but as I tried, he held my chin so I couldn't move.

"If you really think that I am going to let you disappear again, then you are sorely mistaken." He let go of my chin, a mischievous grin spreading across his face. "You still owe me a wedding." This time I scoffed. Yeah fucking right pal. Without saying another word, he closed the door and I've never backed the car out so quickly. Holy fuck, I did not like the way that man made me feel.

CHAPTER SIX

As I downed my 4th gin and tonic in a span of 20 minutes, I felt the room start to spin. My face was getting increasingly hotter by the second and suddenly the people around me were starting to make me feel claustrophobic. I managed to mumble out some version of 'I'm going to step outside'. It was to no one in particular as I had come to this bar alone in the hopes of erasing what I had just seen in the living room of my family home. It also wasn't helping that my brain was playing on repeat the sounds of Avery's moans to the beat of whatever song was playing in the background. As I stumbled out the back door of the bar, I was clawing at the buttons of my jacket as I felt like it was getting harder to breathe.

"It's not like you guys were ever actually together." Damian pushed away from the brick wall as he spoke, and I jumped to the side as I hadn't realized he was standing there. "It was just going to be an arranged marriage. Although, I can understand why my brother would choose Avery over you." It took me a minute in my drunken state to register what he had said before I angrily turned toward him.

"What is that supposed to mean?" I slurred.

"The Blackwood family have always been weak, but you are truly pathetic. At least if he picked Avery our father wouldn't be completely disappointed that he has to marry one of you." I hadn't realized that as he spoke, he stepped closer to me, his cobalt blue eyes filtered through the shaggy blond hair in his face, and they were filled with hatred as he looked at me. "You are nothing, Arabella."

"Fuck you, Damian." As I said it, I watched his face twist into something almost demonic. I felt my back hit the wall hard, nearly knocking all the breath out of me. My head bounced off the stone as his hands slid around my neck, tightening more with every second.

"It should be mine." His voice snaked its way into my ears as he pressed me further between the wall and his hard body. I quickly sobered up, although my vision was beginning to go in and out and I realized if I didn't fight back, I was going to die.

I lunged forward in the hotel room bed, my phone screaming from a call by an unknown number, and I had never been more grateful to be woken up. It turned out to be the lady from yesterday, Silva I later learned, and she gave me the last known location of the first person on the list; Alexei Sokolov. And surprise, surprise it just so happened to be Keiran's club. Fucking fantastic.

She gave me a few other details about him. Mostly that he regularly hired Fiends for different jobs and was involved in trafficking Mercenaries and selling them to said Fiends to feast on. He even had a large clientele of humans that he sold Mercenaries to so that they could use their Auras. Which is highly against the rules if The Spiral found out about it. Part of the pact between us and the humans was that our abilities were off limits to them after they nearly wiped us out during what they called the Witch Trials. Unless, of course, they could pay top dollar for objects that are infused with our Aura. But they are not allowed to have it from the source and most of the human population is not supposed to know we still exist. As far as they were concerned, the earth was rid of the Mercenaries and their evil ways. So, this guy was a shit bag through and through.

After she finished giving me the rundown, I jumped in the shower. I threw on some black yoga pants and my hoodie, added a little mascara and blush to give the illusion I wasn't dead inside, and threw my hair up in a messy bun. I then did a quick internet search to find the phone number for Keiran's club.

As much as I hated how the two of us were now intertwined more than I had wanted, I needed to contact him. It would save me so much time if he could just tell me if Alexei really had been there recently and if he knew why. It seemed that I could get more answers out of Keiran if I was honest about what I was doing. So, I was just going to take the L and suck it up.

"Hello?" The lady on the other end of the phone answered quicker than I thought.

"Uh- yeah, hello," I stammered. "I'm looking for Keiran Stark?"

"He's not here." Her tone was rude, almost defensive.

"Well, when will he be in?"

"Who is this?"

"My name is Bella Blackwood."

"O-oh Miss Blackwood, I'm so sorry." she stuttered. "He told me to let him know if you called. I can take your number down so that he can give you a call back." I rolled my eyes.

"If you could please." I gave her my number and after another apology, she hung up quickly. "What an asshole," I said aloud before tossing the phone down beside me again. What was I supposed to do? Just wait around until he decided to call me? I was mentally calling him every unpleasant name I could think of when my phone started ringing. It was unknown again, so I figured it'd be another one of Alexander's guys.

"Arabella." His tone already seemed angry as Keiran said my name.

"Just as charming as ever," I replied. I expected a retort, but he ignored it.

"I'm texting you an address. Meet me there."

"Why? So you can intimidate me into giving you all my secrets?"

"I'm assuming you called looking for me because you needed my help. I'm a busy man, Miss Blackwood, so you are going to have to come along with me if you want me to answer your questions."

"Are you going to be grumpy again the whole time?"

"I wasn't grumpy last night."

"If you say so." I probably shouldn't have taunted him if I needed his help. "Fine. I'll meet you there." He didn't even say anything else before he hung up. I pulled up the address after sending him a message telling him that he had such a way with words and headed out the door. I decided to take my car this time in the hopes that I wouldn't feel so exposed again.

As I pulled out of the hotel parking lot, however, I noticed that there was a black sedan that pulled out directly behind me. At first it was just an observation. But as they followed me down the third turn in a row, that paranoia came rushing back. They were too far back for me to see a whole lot of detail, but I was able to make out two males inside of the vehicle. Trying not to panic, I sped up slowly just to see if they would do the same and in a split second I decided to make a quick right. My stomach dropped as they followed suit.

My GPS was already rerouting and told me to make a U-turn at the next light. I did as it instructed, extremely glad that the light turned red by the time they got there. My relief was short lived, however, as they ran the light and flipped around. I sped up again, this time much quicker and turned back onto the road I had originally been on.

Though it was probably only a couple minutes, it felt like forever when I finally whipped into the parking garage of another hotel, where Keiran told me to meet him. I sped up to the second floor and pulled into the first spot I could find that hid me between other cars. I threw the car into park as I heard the squeal of tires rounding another corner, and ducked down, extremely glad that they hadn't seen where I had gone. I hadn't been aware that I was holding my breath until a loud knock on my window sent me jumping into the passenger seat as I screamed. I met Keiran's amused gaze. I got out of the car quickly, hitting him intentionally with the door as I swung it open.

"What the fuck, Keiran!" He laughed. "That wasn't funny."

"I don't think I've ever heard you scream before. Though, I am curious to know if you knew that you were being followed."

"Oh no shit? I was just living out my hidden dream of being a Nascar racer." I rolled my eyes. "Was that you?"

"Your sarcasm is quite attractive," he said. "But no, that was not me. It means that someone else was having you followed. When did it start?"

"When I left my hotel."

"Where you are alone and unprotected." Now his face was annoyed.

"I can handle myself."

"You nearly jumped out of your skin just now, Arabella because I caught you off guard. Clearly, you were worried about it."

"I do not need your help." That was a lie. That was the

whole fucking reason I was here. His face said as much.

"That may be so, but I would like to help you," he admitted, matter-of-factly.

"Why?"

"Emery said that you were going to be very untrusting."

"There isn't enough time in the day to talk about why that is Keiran," I replied, my voice almost humorous.

"Come upstairs with me."

"Yeah, that'll never happen."

He laughed, "What's the matter? Are you afraid that you might not be as indifferent to me as you think you are?" He stepped closer to me, his toes touching mine. I stepped back, losing my balance and his arm was around my waist. Once again, his touch made everything in me scream. You know you want him, my body taunted. I managed to wiggle free, and he laughed again. "I have to meet with someone inside. I promise I will behave myself."

"Why can't I say no to you?" That smug look fixed itself on his face again.

"I have many theories for that question, several of which I do not think you'd like," he replied as he reached his hand out toward me. Hesitantly, I took it and let him lead me up the stairs and into the building.

I surveyed the place as we walked through the lobby toward the elevator, trying so desperately hard not to focus on the warmth of his hand resting on my lower back. It was incredibly elegant and clean, too clean with its marble floors and pearly white walls. A beautiful chandelier hung high above us, and the light shone brightly against its crystals.

Growing up, I knew of luxury though I had always tried to separate myself from my family name. I had always been dead set on doing everything by myself, accomplishing it on my own so that it couldn't be used against me. Which is why I don't understand why Keiran questioned my never asking for help. Even Alexander never held back when it came to being extravagant, but I still never wanted to be a part of that lifestyle. And so now, I felt incredibly out of place.

"Keiran," I said.

"Arabella," he replied.

"You didn't tell me that there was a dress code. Perhaps I should have worn a Vera Wang instead of yoga pants and a band hoodie. Even you are in a suit, and I look like a bum." All black that fit him nicely and clung to his muscle. I hated how good he looked in it. He laughed as we reached the elevator and hit the button to go up.

"Well, you have a great ass and I prefer the yoga pants, but I can assure you, you look nothing like a bum. You have always been incredibly beautiful." I ignored the comment about my ass but the one about me being beautiful made me blush. I turned away before he could see it and the tinge of sadness it brought. I hadn't thought of myself as beautiful in a long time. In fact, I wasn't sure that I ever really felt that way about myself. Sure, I could dress up and douse myself in makeup but the words that I would never be good enough were always at the back of my mind. Even after I left, Avery made sure to remind me nearly every day through text messages that I never answered, that not only was I reckless and worthless, but that Kieran would never forgive me for what I had done to his brother. She'd taunted that I was ugly inside and out and eventually I just started to believe it. "Where did you go just now?" he asked, pulling me out of my memories. I shook my head as if trying to shake away the thoughts and thankfully the elevator door opened.

"Nowhere," I lied as we stepped onto the landing. I stepped to the side, and he hit the button for the second floor. But as the door closed, I felt a wave of nausea, and everything started to spin. I gripped the bar as the elevator started rising, intensifying my dizzy spell.

"Woah." He caught me as I stumbled forward.

"I'm fine," I replied, my voice shaky.

"No, you aren't," he replied, concern thickening his tone.

"I-I just... don't like elevators." Truth was, I had no idea where it came from. He kept his arm around me, even after we got off, his eyes never leaving me. Was it me or was it extremely hot in this room?

"Keiran." I heard a familiar voice, and my stomach dropped. I turned slowly and at the sight of the four people in front of me, I felt dizzier than I did in the elevator. Looking past the two gray suited bodyguards in front, I met the stoic gray stare of my mother as she crossed her arms over her chest, disappointment in her face.

"What the hell is this?" Avery's shrill voice made me freeze.

"Avery, you haven't seen your sister in five years. Surely, you've got something better to say," my mother's tone was disinterested.

"Not really. She has no right to be here," Avery snapped, her voice cruel. Though it had been five years, she looked almost exactly as she had back then. Her deep blond hair, which came from our father, was cut just above her shoulders and she still had that cynical look in her fierce blue eyes as she pressed her lips in disapproval. Although naturally fit, her physique was toned and looked like she had gotten a fresh tan. Black had always been my color, so she made a point to be the complete opposite and donned bright lively colors in everything she wore.

"I need to go," I said as I tried to push away from Keiran and step back into the elevator. "I can't... this is... too much-" I couldn't make out a coherent response as the room started spinning again. "Keiran-" Before I knew it, everything went black.

****

My eyes fluttered open. I was lying in a bed and the room looked very dim; a thick curtain blocking out the window and it smelt strongly of lavender and vanilla. A familiar scent. But the room was cold, freezing.

I sat up, realizing that I was in nothing but my shirt and panties. Who changed me? I jumped out of the bed, quickly realizing that was a terrible idea as I stumbled forward. Had the bed not been there, I probably would have fallen face first. I steadied myself after a few moments before I went searching for my clothes which were nowhere to be found.

A searing pain shot through my hand and against my better judgment, I cried out. I looked down to see it had been rewrapped. I brought it to my chest, biting back another scream as it throbbed.

"We had to reopen the wound to release the infection." I turned around to find Keiran leaning in the doorway, his eyes on my half naked body.

"Did you take my clothes off?" He shook his head.

"You had a fever, so your mother removed your clothing and turned on the air conditioner to help bring it back down." At that moment my body shuddered as if to prove the point. He pushed away from the door frame and instinctively, I stepped back against the bed. His eyebrows furrowed. "Relax, Arabella." He reached into the drawer on the nightstand beside the bed, pulling my clothes out. I snatched them quickly and started pulling my pants on, desperate for warmth. He watched me, disapproval in his eyes.

"What?"

"Why didn't you mention the wound on your hand?"

"Why didn't you mention that you were going to meet my fucking family?" I replied defensively as I yanked my sweatshirt over my head.

"I didn't think it mattered." He crossed his arms over his chest as he watched me rub my hands up and down my arms and legs, trying to warm them up. Although, my anger toward him would have probably done the trick.

"You think if I wanted anything to do with them, I would have just up and disappeared from their lives as well?" I started looking around for my shoes. I was desperate to get out of there when I realized why the scent was so familiar. I was in my family home and feelings that I was not ready to face were burning beneath my skin, giving me an ounce of the warmth I was seeking.

"I understand why you'd want to avoid Avery and myself. I know full well why you want to avoid your father. But your mother, Arabella? She was devastated when you disappeared."

"Oh yeah I could tell with her deadpan stare and disapproval in her eyes that she was just overcome with emotion when she saw me." I rolled my eyes. "I told you I was just here to do this fucking job."

"This is your home, Arabella."

"Was my home!" I shouted. "It means nothing to me now. None of you mean anything to me now!"

"Arabella-"

"Stop fucking calling me that!" I couldn't find my shoes or my phone, but I didn't care at that moment as I pushed past him and through the bedroom door. I needed to get out of here even though I could feel the dizziness creeping back in again. I made my way down the familiar white painted hallway, filled with pictures of the life I left behind and the nausea was violently fighting its way through me. I was desperately trying to ignore it when my eyes landed on a framed picture of our family and the Stark brothers, Damian in the dead center with my father's arm wrapped proudly around his shoulders.

An involuntary sound broke through my chest as I stumbled forward. Keiran's arm was around me before I hit the ground, but the anxiety mixed with the infection got the better of me as I fainted again.

CHAPTER SEVEN

Keiran

Arabella had slept the entire rest of the day. I hadn't realized how long it had been until my phone chimed with a message from Avery and I looked around to find that her room had grown darker. I had also been preoccupied by trying to figure out the passcode to her phone since it had been going off nearly nonstop since she fainted the first time. The only thing I had managed to do was lock her out of it, which I knew was going to upset her. I just needed something, anything to tell me who had hired her, who it was that she was afraid of.

With a sigh, I quietly left the room and found my way to the kitchen. Though I hadn't been back to this house since that night, I still remembered the layout well. I spent most days of my childhood here, desperately seeking the warmth of a family that cared. Though Jezebel had been stoic in seeing her daughter for the first time in so many years, she loved her children more than anything and I knew what those five years had done to her. The only thing we knew was that Damian had attacked Arabella and she had killed him before disappearing and not knowing if her daughter had lived or died had nearly driven her insane.

I found her in the kitchen, her sad eyes staring down at

the cup sitting on the table. Her slightly withering hands were folded, resting in front of her and her jet-black hair, specked with silver flakes, was pulled to one shoulder.

"Jezebel." My voice was soft as I took the seat beside her so as not to startle her out of her thoughts. She looked up and smiled though it didn't quite reach her eyes.

"You must be starving after watching over her all day. Let me make you something." She started to stand up, but I put my hand over hers.

"There's no need. I'm not hungry." She slumped back down in her chair. She always needed to feel like she was doing something. It's how she kept her mind from thinking of all of the bad things that have happened. I first noticed it after my mother, her best friend, had died and that was when I started spending most of my time here. Of course, that was also partially due to the fact that I was obsessed with her youngest daughter's ability to see past my bullshit. We were quiet for a moment.

"Avery has left," she said. I nodded.

"That's probably for the best. Fighting is the last thing she needs right now." She turned toward me and that was when I saw the tears in her eyes. A sob escaped her lips, and I embraced her in a hug as she broke down.

"I thought she was dead, Keiran." I had searched for Arabella every day since she had disappeared. Every so often I'd get a hit, a little information about someone that fit her description enough to make me think it could have been her. But every time I went to investigate, there was no sign of her and as much as it pained me to think about it, there was a large part of me that believed that the reason it never turned out to be her was because she died that night. That she crawled away from her fight with Damian only to be killed my some filthy fucking Necro. It ate me up inside every day for the last five years, but I never voiced that opinion because I didn't want her to feel the same.

"But she didn't. And now she is here," I tried to sound upbeat.

"Though she seems determined to leave." No longer crying, she sat up, wiping the tears from her face. "I do not want her to leave, Keiran... I can't handle it again." The last part was a whisper, but I heard it loud and clear.

"I do not plan on letting her go this time." As I said it, I heard the light click of a closed door. Jezebel's eyes shut up with just a semblance of hope as she stood up and I followed her down the hallway. Arabella was nearly out the front door, barefoot and her fingers on the handle as Jezebel spoke.

"Please don't go." Jezebel's voice was soft, almost pleading and I watched the turmoil in Arabella's eyes as she saw and heard the emotion in her mother's voice. "Please, Arabella." A look of pain crossed her face, like she was fighting every instinct in her body to turn and run to her mother. She had always been stubborn whether it was arguing with her sister, pissing off her father, or challenging me to a sparring match that always ended up with her losing. But she was always the most stubborn when it came to being vulnerable and she'd avoid it at every cost.

"I can't," she said, the promise of tears just on the end of her tongue.

"Why not?" I asked finally, fighting my own internal battle to run to her. "Your whole life was here, Arabella."

"A life that no longer exists," she said as she turned for the door again.

"It's safer if you stay here," Jezebel said quickly, her hand going up as if she were going to stop her if she had to.

"Someone was following you," I added. "Until we know why, I don't think that you should be staying by yourself."

"Until I know why," she retorted, over-pronouncing the

word "I" as she looked at me, annoyed. "And I can just switch hotels."

"Or you can stay here where you are safe." She rolled her eyes, but I watched her options play out in her head. Even if she didn't agree, I would have found the hotel she was staying at and booked the room next to her to make sure no one came after her. I was just as hard-headed as she was. Probably even worse.

"I'll only stay on three conditions," she said finally. "One is that you take down the picture with Damian in the hallway. Two, keep Avery the hell away from me." I watched the pain cross Jezebel's face again, but she nodded. "And the other is that you stay the hell out of my business. Thanks for locking me out of my phone by the way." I shrugged my shoulders, an innocent grin lifting the corner of my mouth.

"You kept getting messages and I wanted to know why you think you will be in deep shit if you don't find the amulet." Jezebel's gaze shot back to me and then to her daughter again.

"What amulet?" Arabella shook her head, her eyes throwing me daggers.

"Oh, I'm still not spilling all my secrets, even if you tell my mother, Keiran." I laughed and held up my arms like I was innocent. Defeated, she walked back towards us, moving past me with a forceful push. "I think I've had enough catching up for one night."

CHAPTER EIGHT

It hadn't been hard to figure out which hotel she had been staying at. When she left the diner the other day, she left on foot which meant that she had to have been staying close by. Thankfully, there was only one hotel that was even remotely near that location. When I got there, I was greeted by the friendly smile of the young man behind the concierge counter.

"Good morning, Sir. Are you checking in?"

"No actually," I replied. "I was wondering if you could help me. A friend of mine was staying here but we have found her another arrangement and I need to pick up her things. I was wondering if you'd be able to allow me to do so?" His gentle smile fell into a frown as he knitted his eyebrows.

"I'm really not supposed to do that," he admitted, apology in his voice.

"I do understand the concern. If it would make you feel better, you are more than welcome to accompany me in the room. I truly just wish to grab her things." I watched the turmoil roll around in his head as he contemplated it. I reached into my pocket, pulling out a couple large bills just to sweeten the deal. "I'd make it worth your while." His hazel eyes grew wide as he took in the money I placed down on the counter before he looked back and forth, checking to make sure no one else was watching.

"Wh- what was the name on the reservation?"

"Arabella or possibly Bella Blackwood." I watched as he quickly typed the name into his computer before looking back up at me with a frown.

"I don't have a reservation under that last name. I do have a Bella Stark though." I couldn't help the grin that appeared on my face.

"That's the one."

"Okay. She's staying in room 102." I slid the money over to him as he handed me a key card.

"One more thing if you can. Can you tell me if the name on the form of payment is different from the name on the reservation?" He turned back to the computer, the sound of him hitting the keys, the only sound in the room. He shook his head.

"It just lists her name as the card holder." Damn it.

"Do me a favor and keep the reservation open. If anyone comes asking for her, just say that she stepped out for the day." I pulled out another large bill and slid it over to him and he grinned widely.

"You got it, boss."

"Thanks for the help." I turned and headed for the elevator.

Bella Stark. Clever. No one would think to look up the name because it didn't exist. At least not yet.

Before everything had turned into what it did, Arabella was supposed to be my wife. Strong Mercenary bloodlines were few and far between and arranged marriages were not unusual. Her parents had promised one of them to either myself or Damian, and since Damian hated that idea with a fucking passion, I was going to be the one to do it. Arabella had been my best friend, my closest confidant, the one person who made me feel something again after my mother had died. Not to mention I had wanted her since the moment we met. So, I was more than willing to make her my wife when the time came. We just never got that far. But the fact that she chose that last name made me smile. A person can change a lot in five years but despite what she said, this town and those of us in it, did still mean something to her.

I reached the room quickly and ducked inside. The smell of her hit me hard, so I knew it was the right room, but there wasn't much for me to grab. Apart from a duffel bag, its clothing contents splayed across the bed, some make up, a phone charger, her shoes, and a folded up piece of paper on the nightstand, the room was pretty empty. Was this what her life had been reduced to?

Ignoring my heavy guilt, I neatly packed all her things into the duffel bag. I was going to throw away the paper when a gnawing feeling hit me hard in the chest to check it. Might as well add it to the list of things she was angry at me for. I unfolded the paper to find a list of names.

Alexei Sokolov

The Spider

Keiran Stark

I'd assumed this is a list of people who could have anything to do with the Cursed Amulet. The fact that she managed to get enough information to narrow it down to the three of us was almost alarming. Because they weren't exactly names that were thrown around lightly. The Cursed Amulet wasn't even a term that people used loosely. At least not as of late. So, why was her boss having her hunt it down? How did she even get in this situation to begin with? There were so many questions that I had running through my head as I tucked the list into my pocket. It's not like she'd tell me what was going on in that beautiful brain of hers. Prying it out of her was going to be harder than trying to get her to trust me again. And that was feeling impossible at the moment.

I could feel the physical tension in my shoulders as I drove, my knuckles turning white as they gripped the steering wheel. Though I kept my eyes on the road in front of me, my mind was clearly elsewhere. There was no way in hell I'd be able to convince her to give up whatever it is she was sent here to do. So instead, I realized that my best bet was to indulge her. Using the touch screen on my dashboard, I hit the call button under Liam's name.

"Hey boss," he answered on the fourth ring, his Irish accent sounding slightly winded. "Sorry. I was... occupied." I rolled my eyes, realizing exactly why he sounded so out of breath.

"Please don't tell me you left whatever poor woman you are with right now unsatisfied to answer this phone call." His laugh was sinister.

"I'd never leave a beautiful woman unsatisfied. Now me on the other hand... I've got blue balls so bad I might need your help to relieve myself later." His laugh was boisterous as I scoffed.

"You're a beautiful man, Liam but you aren't my type."

"Ow, you wound me, Stark." I responded with a laugh of my own but continued.

"I need you to bring Alexei Sokolov's file to the club. You can leave it in my desk drawer if I'm not there as I've got to stop by the Blackwood home first." I heard the slight confusion in his tone.

"Uh, sure thing boss. I thought you, uh, stayed away from that house."

"It's... complicated."

"Does this complication possibly go by the name Arabella Blackwood?" Emery couldn't keep her mouth shut to save her life. I sighed, frustrated. "Hey man, I'm assuming since you haven't been banned from the place that it's going better than you thought it would."

"It's a rocky situation," I answered honestly. "She hasn't chopped my dick off yet so I guess it could be worse."

"I'm sure there are a few things you'd like her to do with your dick, man."

"Okay, Liam," I said, exasperated. "Just because you fuck every woman within 2 hours of being around her, doesn't mean that everyone else does too."

"Hmm women are beautiful creatures, Keiran. I don't just fuck them. I worship them."

"I'm hanging up now." I heard his distant laugh through the speaker before it was cut short by my ending the call. That man was the biggest horn dog I had ever met. I had my fair share of women. Of course, it was trying to fill a void that was never going to be filled by mindless sex. But that man fucked just to fuck.

CHAPTER NINE

Arabella

I didn't think I could sleep as deep as I did that night. I don't know if it was lingering effects from the infection or from the emotional exhaustion from last night, but I passed out within minutes of laying down and didn't wake until well into the morning. I probably could have slept longer but my bladder was screaming at me, and the smell of bacon filled my nose. With a full body stretch, I got out of the bed and stumbled to the bathroom.

My reflection in the mirror was almost horrifying. My hair was a tangled mess, and I never washed the makeup off my face, so it was beginning to smear. I turned the shower on quickly and stripped down. The burning hot water felt phenomenal on my skin, and I probably could have stayed standing there beneath it until the water ran out. But I used the face wash that was on the shelf and scrubbed my face until I no longer looked like a raccoon before washing my hair and body.

When I got out of the shower though, I realized that I didn't have anything to change into. Thankfully, there was a giant oversized towel folded neatly underneath the sink and I used it to dry my body and hair before wrapping it around myself tightly. I silently pleaded that Keiran was nowhere to be found as I made my way to the kitchen and found my mother with her back toward me, cooking that delicious smelling food.

"I'm sure you are hungry," she said as she turned around, a giant smile on her face as she reached to place a cup of coffee in front of me. As if the last 5 years weren't hanging between us.

"Starving," I admitted. "But I actually didn't have anything to wear." I took a sip of the piping hot drink.

"I mean the towel looks great." I looked up as Keiran walked into the room, my duffel bag that I had brought with me to the hotel in his hand as he chuckled. I rolled my eyes, turning my gaze back down so that he didn't see my blush as he set the bag down on the oak kitchen table.

"How did you get that?" I asked, snatching it up and pulling it to me, as if that could block his view of me.

"I have my ways." His smile was seductive. I rolled my eyes again. "I also found this." He held up the list of three names that Alexander had given me, and my anxiety spiked. "When I saw my name, I was hoping it was a list of people that you admire but then when I saw the other two, I was very disappointed." His tone was joking but I could tell by the way he looked at me, he was upset. He knew exactly what it was, and I didn't know how I was going to lie my way out of this one. I tried to snatch it from him, but he pulled it back so that I'd have to lean against him to grab it. But I wasn't going to bite.

"Just let her eat, Keiran, before you start asking her questions. She is far too thin," my mother said as she placed a large plate of food in front of me. Eggs and bacon with a hash brown patty and 2 slices of sourdough bread. She gave me a small smile and I could still see the tears that she was fighting. I dropped my gaze back down to the table.

"Thank you," I said and started eating. I really was hungry. It had been days since I had a proper meal. My stomach groaned in agreement.

"You too sir. Just because you are Proctor does not mean that you can't have a home cooked meal sometimes." My eyes shut up in shock. The Proctor was essentially like a governor but for Mercenaries. They held council meetings, upheld the rules, and punished those of us that didn't follow them. Before I left, my father had been Proctor and made no suggestions that he was ready to pass it on. And yet somehow, Keiran now held that title. A lot really did change in five years. "Sit." He did as my mother demanded, taking the chair right next to mine. His knee brushed against mine and I was again made aware that I was in nothing but a towel.

"I need to get dressed," I said, hoping that my face wasn't turning bright red from the interaction.

"Do you have business today?" she asked.

"I've wasted a lot of time," I admitted. She frowned but dropped it quickly in the hopes that I wouldn't notice her offense. But I felt the need to explain. "I have to make a phone call. I'm almost positive my boss is going to want to kill me."

"And why would he want to do that?" Keiran asked after finishing a bite of his eggs. I got up to take my plate to the sink and started to wash it.

"Oh, don't worry about that, Arabella," she said, taking the plate from me. "I just want you to feel comfortable here again." I could tell she really meant it, which made me feel a little guilty for how I spoke to her last night. But I pushed it down and turned back toward Keiran, a look of irritation on my face.

"Don't worry about it." I knew that answer would only frustrate him further as I walked over and grabbed the duffel bag and made my way to the bathroom. I got dressed quickly and went back toward the bedroom where he was leaning in the doorway, watching me with his arms crossed over his chest.

"So, you think I might have the Amulet?" His tone was kind of harsh. I pushed past him to grab my phone. I was just about to put the password in when he snatched it from me. "The people on that list are dangerous, Arabella." I looked up at him defiantly, my eyebrow raised.

"So, you're dangerous too Mr. Proctor?" The way he looked me up and down like he wanted to devour me made me take a step back. "I'll take that as a yes." I meant for it to sound sarcastic, but my voice was hesitant. I snatched the phone back from him and crossed to the other side of the room to put some distance between us. "I don't think you do. But my boss does."

"Why won't you tell me who your boss is?" His arms were crossed again. And he talked about how I was always defensive.

"Because I'm not allowed to," I admitted.

"Why not?" I pressed my lips, as if the answer to that question wasn't fucking obvious.

"Because he, too, is dangerous, Keiran. You think powerful people just go around showing everyone their hand?"

"Is that where you learned to throw your Aura at your opponent without having to touch them? Emery told me what you did to those hunters. She hasn't shut up about it." I narrowed my eyes.

"I was saving her life and as you can see, they still almost killed me." I waved my bandaged hand in front of me. "If he had seen that I never would have lived it down." He shook his head.

"If he is so powerful then why couldn't he come for it himself? And why not just run away from him?" I bit my lip, wondering if I should tell him the truth. Fuck it, he already knew too much. With a sigh, I held out my right forearm and gently ran my left thumb across it. Slowly, the Bind became visible, an intricate line of ancient runes that Alexander had placed on me. "You didn't." He gently grabbed my arm, running his rough fingers along the markings. "Why, Arabella?" I pulled my arm away from him before hiding the Bind again.

"I was reckless," I admitted. "I stole from him because I needed to get a life away from here. At the time I didn't know that he was the one I stole from." I sat down on the bed, recalling the night that I met Alexander. "I had nowhere to go or anyone to turn to."

"You could have come to me," he replied angrily.

"I was too afraid," I admitted.

"Why?"

"Because after what I did-" I trailed off. No. No vulnerability, Arabella. "It doesn't matter. I had no other option except to leave and I just so happened to steal from the wrong fucking person. Now, this is what I owe him for sparing my life."

"Do you think that I would have taken his side?" he asked after what felt like an eternity. "Do you really think that I would have chosen him over you?"

"We don't have to talk about that," I said. "I was only telling you what I was thinking when I did what I did."

"Eventually we have to talk about it, Arabella." Back was my defensive attitude as I stood up from the bed.

"I told you to stop calling me by my full name," I snapped. "Now, if you are done being a pain in my ass, I need to check my messages." He sighed and I knew there was so much more he wanted to say but thankfully he didn't press the issue as he left me alone in the room again.

Finally, I was able to open my phone and nearly lost it when I saw the number of messages from Alexander that I had missed. He really was going to kill me. I tried to call him, thinking that he would pick up on the first ring like he usually did when he was angry with me. But he didn't. In fact, he didn't answer me at all. Not even the message that I tried sending him, letting him know what happened, though not telling him where I was. It was nice that no one knew where I was because then I wouldn't have to worry about being watched by him or his people. But it worried me that he wasn't responding.

Ignoring the pit in my stomach from the situation, I went back out to find Keiran. After all, this whole situation happened because I needed his help. Though he may be pissed at me now. But I didn't have another option. He obviously knew the other 2 people on the list because he knew they were dangerous and at least one of them had visited his club. So, I had to suck it up.

I found him in the kitchen, offering a consoling shoulder to my mother as she cried. Though she tried to hide it as I walked in by turning back toward the kitchen sink, picking up a dirty plate to clean it off. I didn't acknowledge it though. One, because I didn't want her to feel embarrassed but also because Keiran was right, and these were conversations that I would have to have. But they were going to be on my terms and right now, I didn't have the luxury.

"Are you still willing to help me?" I asked him.

"Well, if I am being honest, Arabella-" He emphasized my name just to irritate me, "-What if what you find is not at all what you were expecting?" I shrugged.

"Wouldn't be the first time I was severely underwhelmed."

CHAPTER TEN

I stayed silent for the most part in the car ride over to his club. The scene in the kitchen was eating me alive. It wasn't long before my thoughts got the best of me.

"Was she crying because of me?" I asked finally, breaking the silence. He kept his eyes on the road ahead of us but the way his hands tightened on the steering wheel, I knew I wasn't too far off.

"In a way," he admitted. "She was crying for you."

"Because of the Bind?" He only nodded. "She didn't need to know that." My tone was defensive.

"I didn't tell her. She overheard us talking." I sighed and pinched the bridge of my nose.

"This is a mess." I wasn't really speaking to him, just thinking out loud.

"Did you think it would go smoothly?" I shook my head.

"Honestly, I thought that I wouldn't run into any of you. I told my boss that I could handle this. That this town and the people in it meant nothing to me anymore. Clearly, the Gods had other plans."

"Is that really so bad?" This time he looked between me and the road. "To learn that maybe the situation was not what you thought it was?"

"Why is it just on me though? Why am I the one that was in the wrong?"

"You weren't. That's the whole point." He had grown quiet, and I thought that he was lost in thought but then I realized it was because we had stopped moving. We were now parked in front of the club. I got out of the car quickly as I was starting to feel suffocated, and he followed suit. Thankfully, he didn't continue the conversation as I followed him inside.

It was brightly lit up, no flashing lights, or pulsing gothic music as a tall slender Korean woman with neon pink hair and thick iron bracelets clashing around her wrists, danced around the room with a broom, completely unaware that we were standing there. Keiran chuckled which startled her, and she dropped the thing, the wooden handle making a loud clanging noise as it hit the floor.

"I'm so sorry, Keiran. I didn't know you'd be in so early. Otherwise, we would have had it a lot cleaner."

"Oh, he'll get over it," I heard Emery call from behind one of the booths. I looked up as she came barreling towards us, as energetic and giddy as she could be. "Hey Bella!" She tried to hug me, but I held up my arms to try and stop her.

"I'm not a hugger," I offered. She rolled her eyes and slammed her arms around me anyway, a giant smile on her face. Keiran laughed again.

"The sooner you give in, the sooner she stops," he replied. I huffed out an annoyed sigh and hugged her back quickly. With a giggle, she let go and skipped back toward where she had been to finish whatever she had been doing.

"You know child labor laws are a thing," I joked as I

followed him toward the back of the building, to his office I'm guessing. He laughed.

"She's technically an adult. But I'm not forcing her to do anything. She said she enjoys helping clean this place because she finds money and other 'cool things'." He used his fingers to make quotation marks around his words. "I just let her do it."

"Is the girl with the pink hair a human?" I asked, noting that I couldn't sense her Aura. He shook his head.

"She used to be a Mercenary." I saw a look of pain cross his face though he tried to hide it. I looked at him, confused. "Those iron bracelets are infused with some of my Aura. But she herself does not have her power anymore."

"Why not?" We had reached a large oak door, and he pulled a key from his pocket to unlock it. Once we were inside, he closed it quickly before continuing.

"Her whole family was slaughtered when she was younger and just because he could, the Mercenary that did it, ripped her Aura from her."

"Another Mercenary did that to her?" He nodded.

"She tried to kill me," he admitted, clearly lost in the memory as I watched him. "She wanted me dead as payment for my father killing her family."

"YOUR father?"

"Can't say that I blamed her. He was a fucking asshole." Despite us growing up together, I had never met his father. I had only heard stories about how he had beaten and tortured Keiran so that he would be just like his older brother. So that he would be the killer that his father was. Keiran was ruthless, emotionless when it came to protecting those around him. I had witnessed it many times not only while training with him but also while fighting demons on more than one occasion. But there was also a side to him that no one else saw unless he wanted you to, and his father hated that about him. Hated that he had compassion for those that were considered 'weaker' than him. And then when he abandoned his sons only months before the death of their mother, it no longer mattered. "So, Sakura became one of us."

"It seems you have a knack for picking up strays," I said with a laugh as he reached into the drawer of his mahogany desk. He pulled out a large manilla envelope and placed it down in front of me; the name Alexei Sokolov written on the front of it.

"I always preferred them to the rest of society." I picked it up and opened it, pulling out a thick stack of paper. "And beings like Alexei Sokolov are the reason why." I only skimmed through the first few pages and was disgusted by that alone. Not only was he the largest trafficker in Hallowed Haven of both humans and Mercenaries alike, but he also sold and traded the corpses of the demons that his men would capture and kill as some form of a trophy. Hunted beings for sport and displayed them with pride. As I flipped through page after page of pictures of his 'possessions' I wanted to vomit. I closed it quickly and set it back down on the table.

"Why would you allow him to come in here?" I asked.

"Because I too was gathering information on him. You'd be surprised what things people will admit when they are surrounded by beautiful men and women and full of alcohol."

"Why?"

"Because I have been assigned to assassinate him."

"Assigned?" He raised an eyebrow. "What does that mean, Keiran?" He took a deep breath and watched me closely for what felt like forever before responding.

"You are not the only one who aligned themselves with terrible bedfellows to get what they wanted, Arabella." It took me a second but when I realized what he meant, my eyes went up in shock.

"Did you become a member of the Spiral?" He sat back in his chair, his intense stare never leaving mine, giving me all the answers I needed. That also explained how he was able to hold the title of the Proctor as well. "Why Keiran?"

"Just as there are things that you will not share with me yet, there are things that I will not share with you." His tone was harsh again, warning me without saying not to press the issue further.

"So, you are going to kill him," I continued, dropping it. "What if he has the amulet?"

"He doesn't."

"How do you know?" A strange look crossed his face quickly but was gone just as fast.

"The amulet is an immense source of power that very few would be able to contain. Despite what he may have people think, he is not that powerful. He relies heavily on magical objects in any fight he encounters. Not to mention the Fiends he sometimes hires so that he doesn't have to do anything himself." I bit my lip, thinking about it for a moment. I suppose that knocks a name off the list. But Keiran was going to kill him... Almost as if he could hear my thoughts he said, "He will be here tonight."

"And you're going after him? Won't he have a bunch of his people around him? That could be dangerous."

"Are you worried about me, Arabella?" Back was that seductive smirk. I rolled my eyes, trying to act like I still wasn't affected by him.

"No. I hope he kicks your ass since you won't stop calling me by my real name." I crossed my arms over my chest.

"You have a beautiful name. I don't understand why it

bothers you now." Because it reminds me of the past. But I didn't say that.

"It doesn't. I just don't like the way that YOU say it." His laugh was genuine.

"If you say so, Arabella." I rolled my eyes. This was a losing battle.

"Anyway, I'd like to be there when you do it."

"Absolutely not." I pressed my lips, annoyed.

"Excuse me?"

"As you said, it'll be dangerous. I'm not putting you in that situation."

"You wouldn't be," I defended. "I'd be putting myself in that situation." This time he was annoyed.

"It's the same thing, Arabella. Alexei is a vile man, and you are exactly the type that he would go for. I do not want you to get hurt."

"I'm not some fragile little thing. You can't stop me." He crossed his arms over his chest and just stared at me, his gaze intimidating. I slightly leaned back, a little uncomfortable as I felt like his gaze was burning me again. "You don't want me there because it's dangerous, but you can be there by yourself?"

"I won't be by myself," he offered. "Avery will also be there." As much as I hated to admit it, I felt a ping of disappointment when he said my sister's name and unwanted images of the two of them together flooded my stupid brain. He knit his eyebrows together as he looked at me. Sometimes my face gave away my thoughts without me even trying. "What?" I shook my head and stood up.

"Why waste my time bringing me here then? You could have just told me that and I could have moved on to the next name on the list." I walked away, hoping that he didn't see the embarrassment on my face.

"Wait," he called after me. "What just happened?"

"Nothing," I lied. "All of this has been a giant waste of time and I'm still no closer to getting this stupid thing off of me. I never should have asked you for help." I ignored his call for me to come back. I even acted like I couldn't hear Emery calling for me as I ran out of the building. I ran down the side streets, my anxiety fueling my every move.

Was it anxiety? Anxiety because I had very little information to give Alexander? Anxiety because he still hadn't replied back to me, and I knew he was fucking pissed? Or was it the embarrassment I felt because I was jealous of my sister and Keiran? That was the whole reason I ended up in this very fucking situation. I was jealous that Keiran didn't choose me.

"Fuck!" I yelled, out of breath as my running came to a stop. I felt so stupid as I hunched over, placing my hands on my knees as I tried to catch my breath. I was nearly hyperventilating so I hadn't felt him come up behind me. A large hand was around my mouth before I could react. I heard Alexander's laugh before I saw him walk out from the darkened alleyway to the left of me. My panic attack came to a full head as I thrashed against the person holding me.

"Taylor is more than twice your size, Arabella. You can't get out." Alexander said, his voice almost maniacal. Taylor's grip tightened as he said it, cutting off my breathing completely as he kicked my legs out from underneath me. I fell to the ground, my knees hitting hard on the concrete, forcing what little breath I had left out through his clasped fingers. Alexander knelt down in front of me and placed his finger under my chin, forcing me to stare up at him. "I'm going to tell him to let go of your mouth, Arabella. But you better not scream or this time, you will pass out from lack of air. Do you understand me?" I nodded, desperate for a breath. He nodded toward Taylor who finally removed his hand. I inhaled deeply before I started coughing. He grabbed my chin, pinching it between his fingers as he forced my gaze to his again. I bit my lip, fighting the urge to cry out in pain. "I gave you space because you said you can do this. And instead, you disappear? I stopped by the hotel and there wasn't a single trace of you there and the staff knew nothing."

"I didn't," I said through clenched teeth. "I was being followed." This piqued his interest.

"Go on." He let go of my chin but stayed crouched in front of me. I swallowed back the lump in my throat.

"I ran into Keiran Stark." He lifted a brow, amused.

"Ah Keiran," he said with a laugh. "I should have known that the two of you would have found each other. Was he having you followed?" I shook my head.

"I don't know who was following me," I admitted. He made a Tsk sound with his tongue and before I knew what was happening, he grabbed the back of my neck, pulling me up by my hair. I bit down hard on my lip again, drawing blood this time as I fought off a scream.

"You are wasting my time." His voice was angry, his blue eyes nearly black with rage.

"I've crossed one name off of your list!" His eyes widened ever so slightly. "Alexei Sokolov. He doesn't possess the Amulet."

"And how do you know?" His grip tightened and my eyes slid shut to fight the pain.

"He gets most of his power from infused objects and uses Fiends to fight for him. He's not strong enough to wield it."

"Hmm." He thought for a moment before loosening his grip on my hair. "I suppose that is helpful information. But still-" He let go of me completely before Taylor dropped me to my knees again. "You need to be reminded of what happens when you don't follow my rules." He grabbed the arm with the Bind and shot a jolt of his Aura through it. It felt like my flesh was burning from the inside out and this time I whimpered at the pain. Taylor grabbed my neck and forced me to look up at Alexander again as he pushed his long fingernail into the open wound. "Until this is broken, you belong to me, Arabella. Do NOT forget that." He dropped my arm and turned away from me, waving his hand back toward Taylor. As if he was anxiously awaiting the moment, Taylor let go of me just long enough for him to kick me so hard in the stomach that I fell to the ground. I knew I was about to pass out as white spots danced around my vision. The last thing I heard before I passed out was Alexander's chuckle.

CHAPTER ELEVEN

When I came to, I was in excruciating pain. I'm pretty sure that my ribs were broken and to top it off, my arm felt like it was literally on fire.

"Fuck!" I exclaimed as I looked down and saw that the Bind was now burnt into my flesh and completely visible. I pulled the sleeve of my sweater down to hide it, cringing as the fabric brushed against the fresh wound and suddenly, I felt a surge of anger. Not just at Alexander but at every asshole man that thought that I was just going to do what they told me. I made a split decision that I was going to meet Alexei Sokolov no matter what Keiran had to say about it. Right then, I needed a fight.

At least that was what I was telling myself as I made my way back to my family's house. Thankfully, no one was there as I pushed inside and stomped my way to the bathroom to check the damage. As I looked myself over in the mirror, I saw the welt from where he had pinched my chin and whimpered softly as I pulled my sweater up to reveal my badly bruised flesh. Not to mention the burn marks that were still slightly bleeding.

I sighed, which hurt like hell, and went back to the room to search my duffel bag. I pulled the only other dress that I had in my arsenal, a long-sleeved black cocktail dress and stripped out of the clothes I was wearing. I managed to stop the wound from bleeding before I pulled on the dress and was happy that the plunging neckline stopped just short of where the bruising started. It also made my breasts look really good which thanks to Keiran's unnecessary concern, I knew would really get Alexei's attention. I pulled my hair up in a sexy updo to expose my slender neck and did a subtle makeup so that the attention would be drawn to my bright red lips. This time I opted for my boots right away because my intention was for things to go awry.

I took my car this time since I found it in the garage. Keiran must have brought it at some point after I fainted at the hotel. How fucking thoughtful. I rage drove back to his club and the closer I got, the more adrenaline I felt. I also made a last-minute decision when I found the dagger that I had taken from the Hunters that attacked Emery and stuck it inside of my boot.

"This place is always fucking packed," I thought as I made my way through the crowd, hiding the fact that it hurt every time one of them touched me. I think the pain was just fueling me at this point. And as I caught sight of Avery on the second floor, I knew that Alexei was already here.

I managed my way toward the stairs and up to the spacious second floor. I looked around and felt a flutter in my stomach when I saw Keiran sitting in one of the booths. One leg was crossed over the other and the sleeves of his shirt were pulled up to his elbows as they draped over the back of the leather seat. Avery stood beside him in a navy-blue dress that looked more like it belonged on the First lady than someone that frequents this kind of club. She held a tray in her hand with a menagerie of cocktails on it and Alexei sat on the other side of Keiran. His men stood around them, protectively and for a moment I thought that this was really stupid. But my arm twinged in pain again and I forced myself forward. I was just grabbing a half empty drink from another booth when I locked eyes with Keiran. I saw the anger flash in his face, but he couldn't break character as I pretended to stumble into one of Alexei's guards, spilling the drink all over him.

"What the fuck is wrong with you," the guard exclaimed, his Russian accent thick with aggression.

"I'm so sorry," I said slowly as if I were drunk. Keiran stood up quickly and grabbed me by the waist to pull me away, but I cringed. He noticed the movement, looking at me with his eyebrows knit together but I ignored him. "I think I've had too many." I looked to Alexei who was watching me intensely, his brown eyes devouring me possessively. He smiled, a sight that made my skin crawl.

"No need to be sorry," he said, still grinning. "If you come sit here with me, I think that I could forgive you." I smiled sweetly, pushing away from Keiran and pretended to stumble onto Alexei's lap. He laughed, a raspy sound. "I can understand why you retired to own this place, Keiran Stark. Constantly surrounded by beautiful women." Retired? His hand moved to rest high on my thigh and I risked a glance at Keiran. I could see the anger in him seething at my interruption, but I turned to lean into Alexei.

"You seem important," I said with a flirt, running my hands along the buttons of his suit, feeling disgusting having to touch him so intimately. He started to play with the hem of my dress and this time I could feel the energy radiating off Keiran.

"Drunk lonely girls come with the territory," Avery said with displeasure. "Forgive her." Alexei paid her no mind as he spoke to me.

"Yes, I am, Kitten," he purred. I wanted to vomit. "In fact, I was just telling Mr. Stark about my last batch." Finally, he looked up at Keiran. "Some female Mercenaries that were given to us. They were too old of course to be of any value so we decided to play with them instead." I watched him pull a chunky golden chain out from under his shirt and there dangling at the end was what looked like broken teeth. He and his men laughed at the memory of killing them. I felt the anger boil in me again.

"That is so-" I paused, as the smile on my face fell and gone was my flirting tone. "-disgusting." Without hesitating, I stood up and cracked Alexei in the nose. Then, all hell broke loose. As the blood poured from his nose, all four of his men lunged for me.

"Fuck," I heard Keiran say as he grabbed one of them, yanking him back as he too cracked him in the face. Avery launched the alcohol into the face of another and then hit him with the tray that she had been holding. Alexei sat still at the booth as the other two set their sights on me. One stepped behind me and the other in front as they tried to attack me from both sides. I dropped to the ground and kicked out the legs from under the one in front of me before the one behind snaked his hand in my hair and pulled hard.

"Motherfucker," I yelped as I fell back. Instinctively, I elbowed him in his groin.

"Fucking bitch," he seethed as he let go of me and stumbled backward. The one that I had knocked down managed to get back up quickly and grabbed my ankle. I felt his Aura wrapping around my leg like thick vines and I knew that if it kept going higher, I wasn't going to be able to move. Quickly, I reached down and pulled the dagger from my boot and slammed it into the man's cheek before pulling it right back out. He let go of me and grabbed his face, the blood seeping between his fingertips as he cried out. I jumped back up and this time using all the force I had, I slammed the blade into his chest. He fell back and landed hard on the glass table, shattering it.

I had no time to react though as the other reached for me again. I was intending to use my Aura on this one but as his fingers grazed against my skin, Keiran pulled him back, his own Aura wrapping around the man's neck like a black snake. I watched it tighten, cutting his air flow completely until the life drained from his eyes.

Alexei scrambled to stand up, blood still pouring from his nose as he started to run away. This time I threw my Aura to trap him in place and allowed it to burn up around his body, just like the burning feeling that I felt in my arm. Keiran slowly walked up toward him.

"Don't do this," he pleaded. I could see the tears welling up in his eyes as he moved behind him. Keiran bent down and whispered something in his ear, and I watched all the blood drain from his face. "I didn't know. Please don't-" Before he could finish, Keiran wrapped his hands around his neck and snapped it quickly, dropping his large heavy body to the ground with a thud.

CHAPTER TWELVE

Keiran

Watching Alexei touch her was driving me fucking mad. Every time his disgusting fingers grazed her skin, and I watched her physically trying to hide her disgust, I wanted to rip his fucking hands off. But I couldn't break character. I couldn't waste all the time that Avery and I have spent planning this.

When I sought out the Spiral, it was so that I could have every available access to find out what had happened to Arabella. It was so I could gain the power that I needed to protect her. But after so long, I was starting to give up, to lose hope. I had become mindless during my assignments, not taking a single life into consideration as I allowed my anger and aggression to fuel me. Anyone that got in my way was on my shit list and I didn't care how I had gotten it, as long as I got what I wanted. I was acting like the very thing that I hated. My father. So, this was supposed to be my last assignment. My last kill until I could leave, which was not something that was easily done. But in a span of five years, I had taken down more enemies of the Spiral than any before me and I was given the permission to leave once it was finished. And now the woman that started it all, was risking my only chance.

"-Disgusting." I had been so wrapped up in those thoughts and watching Arabella lean back and punch Alexei in the nose, so hard it instantly started bleeding, pulled me back to what was happening. The original plan was to butter him up with alcohol and flattery, two of his favorite things, until I had convinced him that I was interested in buying some of his 'product'. I was going to have him take me to an undisclosed location, giving him the illusion that he was in control, and then take him out. But as all of his men reached for her, I realized we would now have to improvise.

"Fuck," I said as I grabbed one of the men reaching for her and yanked him back toward me and hit him hard in the face. He held his balance though as he threw a punch, trying to infuse it with some of his Aura. I ducked, reaching up and cracking him right in his ribs. He hunched over and I grabbed him by the throat, slamming him backwards onto the ground. He landed hard, knocking the breath out of him and I wasted no time slamming my fist down into his chest, shaping my Aura into sharpened tendrils to pierce into his flesh. He spit up blood before his eyes rolled into the back of his head and he died quickly.

The loud sound of shattering glass pulled my attention back to Arabella. One of the men who she had taken on was lying dead with a blade that reeked of poison sticking out of his chest and the other was reaching for her again. I wrapped the tendrils around his neck, tightening faster the more he tried to pull away from me until he too was lifeless on the ground.

Alexei groveled forward, desperately trying to get away. Arabella threw her Aura at him, its dark red hue encircling him and capturing him where he stood so that he couldn't escape. But this one was mine and he knew it as I walked up to him.

"Don't do this," he pleaded, the tears streaming down his greasy face. I bent down so that I was at ear level with him.

"You thought you could put your hands on my wife, and I wouldn't kill you?" As I said it, we both looked toward Arabella, and I could feel the panic eating him alive.

"I didn't know. Please, don't-" I snapped his neck, dropping his worthless body to the ground before looking back at her. She looked around, surprised by the fact that no one in here was reacting to the bodies that lay at our feet. My employees knew better and any Fiend that was close enough to know what was happening, was too engrossed in the depravity of humanity to care.

"What the fuck is wrong with you." My voice was angry as I watched her viciously pull the blade from the man's chest and wiped its contents on his clothing before hiding it back inside of her boot.

"You could have ruined this whole thing," Avery sneered, the distaste for her sister clear on her face.

"I don't like being told what to do." She said it with such a bitter laugh as she stepped around the bodies, aiming to just leave after what just happened. I grabbed her by the waist and watched her contort in pain. It was the second time she had done that.

"Were you hurt?" I asked, not caring how desperate I sounded. She only shook her head and tried to pull out of my grasp again.

"Not from the fight. You were going to kill him anyway." I shook my head, the anger I felt building more and more as she acted like it was nothing.

"That's not the point." I grabbed her arm to keep her from trying to leave again and this time she cried out. No longer believing that she was fine, I pulled up her sleeve to reveal the Bind, bleeding and burnt into her skin. "What the fuck is that?"

"Like I said, I don't like being told what to do." She

shrugged.

"Your boss did this to you? He put his fucking hands on you?" I didn't think I could hate this fucker even more than I already did and I didn't even know who he was yet. But when I found out, I was going to personally fucking bury him.

"Wouldn't be the first time," she admitted, like it was no big fucking deal. I felt my jaw flex, the anger in me boiling to a dangerous level. "Are we going to clean this up or what?" The look on my face must have been something as I watched her take a step back, trying to close in on herself as she often did when she was trying to be invisible. Oh, baby girl, you take up far too much space, just in my psyche alone, to be invisible.

"No." I pulled my phone out of my pants pocket and dialed Liam's number for the second time today. This time he answered right away.

"Taking me up on my offer?" he said with a laugh. I was too angry to reciprocate.

"I need you to meet me at the club."

"Ah a bad night, eh? Did you not get your target?" He always asked that after he knew I was dealing with an assignment even though he knew damn well that I'd never allow someone to live if they were my target.

"Just get here quickly, Liam."

"Alright, alright. You're always so bossy and demanding." I hung up, not saying another word as I looked back at her.

"I'm going to have Liam take you back home." She rolled her eyes.

"I drove here. I don't need anyone to take me back. I just want to clean up my mess and leave."

"You aren't touching them," I snapped. "That's the Spiral's job as they have to have proof that he is dead." She cringed, though I wasn't sure if it was from the pain or the guilt that crossed her face. "And I'm not fucking arguing with you. I'll drive your car back to the house later." She put her hand on her hip, defiance clear on her face.

"Yeah? And maybe I want to argue with you and this incessant need to fucking protect me. I'm not yours, Keiran." Before she had finished her statement, I was already in front of her. She took a step back, a moment of panic fleeting in her eyes before she stood her ground as I looked down at her.

"You can argue that all you want, baby. But you're mine and if you don't leave, I will throw you over my fucking shoulder and carry you out myself." She knit her eyebrows together in frustration.

"You wouldn't dare." I smiled cruelly as I bent down and picked her up, noting how light she felt with a frown, before tossing her gently on my shoulder.

"Keiran!" She screamed as she tried to use one hand to cover her ass and the other pressed against my back to hold herself up. "What the fuck is wrong with you!"

"Damn did I miss all the fun?" I turned around and found Liam standing there with his arms on his hips, fanning false upset.

"I need you to take this one back to Jezebel's house for me."

"Put me down, asshole! Or I'll fucking scream." I laughed.

"You've been here enough times now to know Arabella that the people here wouldn't see a scream as an alarm."

"Fine," she sighed, defeated. "I'll go. Just put me down." I shook my head, though I couldn't help but picture how red her cheeks probably were right now and started toward the stairs.

"Too late now, love. Should have went when I gave you the chance." I looked back at Avery who seemed genuinely pissed about the whole thing.

"Call Elysium and let him know that it's done, and his men can come collect. I'll be back in a minute." Despite her trying to fight with me both physically and verbally, I kept her on my shoulder the whole time as I walked through the club and outside to Liam's shitty white Toyota. All the money I paid this man for being my right hand and putting up with my shit and he still refused to buy himself a better car. As he hit the button on his fob to unlock it, I set her down in the passenger seat. She kicked her leg out, trying unsuccessfully to kick me in the balls and I couldn't help the smile that painted my face.

"You think this is fucking funny, Keiran? I hate you."

"I said that too at first," Liam joked. "But then the bastard grew on me. I'm Liam by the way. Thought you should know that." She flipped him off though I knew her anger was at me and not at him. I ducked down in front of her so I could meet her gaze again.

"I can't focus on my job when every time I look at you, I want to go out and scour this city for the bastard that bound you." This time my tone was serious. "So, you can hate me for now if that's what you need. And one day I'll let you take out your aggressions on me, baby but unfortunately tonight's not that night. He's taking you home and don't think for one second that I won't tell him to use restraints if he needs to." Her gaze was deviant again as she crossed her arms over her chest. Gods, she was breathtaking even when she was mad.

"Whatever," she said, turning away from me. "I just want to fucking leave."

CHAPTER THIRTEEN

Arabella

"Keiran is a bit of an arsehole," Liam said after a few minutes of silently driving us toward my mother's house. I scoffed.

"That's an understatement." I could still feel the heat in my cheeks from when he threw me over his shoulder. Although, I couldn't confidently say that the heat was from that and not from what he said about me being his. Or about taking my aggressions out on him...

"But he usually means well," he said, pulling my attention from the need between my thighs. It was fucking pissing me off how much this man turned me on just by looking at me. And then he had to say shit like that and make it worse.

"If that's what you want to call it." He laughed. Liam was quite attractive himself. Even without the freckles, short curly blond hair, and big hazel eyes, his accent I'm sure got a lot of attention. You could also tell that he worked out and was about 5'11 if not 6 foot. "Are you another one of his strays?"

"You could say that, I suppose," he said. "I happened to

be in the wrong place at the right time and he saved my life." I watched the smile that seemed to have been plastered on his face since the club, falter as a memory crossed his mind. "I had a bit of a drug problem, you see. I had been fiending for it and was just round my dealer's flat when I saw a Demon trying to take a little girl. At first, I thought I had fried my brain enough that I was seeing shit until that thing bit right into that girl's neck." He shuddered. "Poor thing couldn't even scream from the blood. You know, I thought I was invincible or something. I don't know. So I ran toward her. If Keiran hadn't shown up when he did, neither of us would have made it." He paused for a moment and back was that chipper smile. "Anyway, he helped me off the stuff. Gave me a job, gave me a purpose and here I am."

"Can I be honest with you, Liam?" I asked.

"Of course, luv," he said, looking back and forth between me and the road.

"That makes me hate him even more." This time he laughed.

"Keiran is a powerful, brutal man. Except when it comes to those that are broken. I think he sees that he is the same so wants to be there for those in a way that no one was there for him." I knew this about him. He had always been that way, and I was beginning to think that maybe he saw me as one of those broken things that he could fix. Well maybe I liked my pieces. Maybe those pieces were the only things that kept me moving for the last 5 years and I wasn't ready to let them go yet.

I was still in my head by the time we made it back to the house. My mother was there waiting to heal me as Keiran had texted her right after we left the parking lot, thankfully not giving her any details about everything that happened that night. And as much as I didn't want to admit it, I was grateful as the pain was starting to become unbearable as my adrenaline wore off. I was ready to curl up into a ball by the time I made it inside the house. My mother had some of the best healing abilities that our kind had ever seen and she had already started using it from the moment she touched me.

"My Aura isn't quite as good as it once was so I can't remove the burn marks," she admitted as we sat beside each other on the couch, her energy pulsing through my broken ribs like a tens unit.

"It's fine. It's my fault anyway," I said lazily, my eyes half open as I tried to relax. A small sob escaped her, and I opened my eyes to see the tears falling from hers.

"It isn't though," she said, through tears. I felt awkward and unprepared for this conversation after tonight's events, but I knew that it was going to have to happen. I sighed.

"It was," I said, turning toward her as I folded my legs underneath me. "I stole from someone that I shouldn't have and now these are the consequences."

"Only because we pushed you away." She finished with my ribs and pulled the shirt that I had changed into back down over my exposed skin. "The bruises will take a day or so to heal because it was pretty bad, but they are no longer broken."

"Thank you." We sat in silence for a few moments. "I don't know how to start this conversation," I admitted. She moved to mirror my sitting position and faced me.

"Just be honest," she said, her face hopeful. I took a deep breath, trying to unscramble my thoughts. "Why did you leave?"

"Straight to the point, huh?" I snorted but she just stared at me eagerly, waiting for me to answer. "There was more than one reason, but I guess I felt ashamed," I admitted. She knitted her eyebrows together.

"Ashamed?" I sighed deeply and thought of how to word the things that were jumbled around in my brain.

"And scared."

"Of Damian?" I shook my head.

"Of Keiran?" She sounded shocked like I was insane for the thought. I shrugged.

"Partly. We were already in some weird fight that night... I honestly thought he had grown to hate me though I wasn't even sure why. And then I found him and Avery... I just- I could only imagine how he'd react when he learned that I killed his brother." I watched guilt flood her face and she shrunk down into herself.

"That was... kind of my fault," She admitted, her voice nearly a whisper.

"What are you talking about?" This time she turned away from me, fidgeting wildly with her hands as she spoke in rushed sentences.

"For the fight between you, I mean. I put too much on him. Asked him for too much."

"What does that even mean?"

"I told him that he couldn't choose you." Her voice was so quiet, if there had been any other hint of sound, I wouldn't have heard what she had said. And it felt like she had knocked all the breath out of me.

"What?" I asked, my own voice nothing more than a whisper.

"I did it to protect you, Arabella." She reached for me, but I pulled away, standing up from the couch. It felt like the pain in my ribs had spread to my entire body as I inhaled sharply.

"From what?" She shook her head.

"From so many things."

"No," I said, my voice louder this time as I felt my anger from earlier returning. "That's not a good enough answer." I could feel the tears stinging my own eyes. "Do you even know what it was like for me? Trying to live up to the Blackwood legacy and constantly being reminded that I was never good enough? He was the one fucking person that understood that. The one person that saw me for me and you and Avery stole that. You can't even imagine how much that fucking hurt. How much it still fucking hurts. And for what? Protection?" As if on cue, the front door opened, Keiran standing in the doorway, his face tired. When he saw the look on my face, it changed to concern.

"What's wrong?" I wiped the tears away quickly, turning away from the both of them.

"Nothing," I lied. I started down the hallway, but he reached for me.

"Would you stop walking away from me?" he said, his voice stern but I could hear the softness behind it. "That's the same thing you did to me this morning and then you show up with broken ribs and fucking burn marks."

"I was just overwhelmed." It wasn't completely a lie. "I'm tired of feeling things that I don't want to. I told you Keiran; I didn't want anything to do with all of this." I threw my hands out. "Even though you may not like it, I'm going to get a few cuts and bruises. I'm not a child." This time I turned to look at my mother, emphasizing the words. "Protection was never what I needed."

CHAPTER FOURTEEN

I don't even remember falling asleep. And apart from the dreams of repeatedly getting kicked in the gut by Taylor, I slept for quite a while. Although, I was sure to send a message to Alexander that Alexei Sokolov had been killed. My sides ached and I didn't want another unannounced visit.

By the time I rolled out of the bedroom, it was the evening time. After a quick shower, I made my way to the kitchen in search of some food to settle my rumbling stomach, hoping that no one else was here. I couldn't face my mother right now. I still had so many questions, but I wasn't going to do it on an empty stomach. I had just decided on some leftover Italian food in the fridge when my cell phone pinged from my pocket. I sighed. I wasn't sure if I had the mental capacity to handle Alexander right now either. I pulled it out anyway. Instead, it was a message from Keiran asking if I was awake yet. I messaged back the word 'No' and set the phone down to take a bite out of my food. His reply was instant.

Him: A woman of many talents. Can even text in her sleep. This time I rolled my eyes before replying.

Me: This isn't Bella. This is just the creep watching her sleep soundly, unbothered by you and your flattery. He didn't reply instantly again so I continued with my food when suddenly the phone rang.

"I'm just trying to enjoy my cold spaghetti," I sighed as I answered it.

"You always did prefer pasta out of the fridge," he laughed. I rolled my eyes.

"Are you calling to give me your Lasagna recipe or was there a reason you were disturbing my peace?"

"Hmm. I keep warning you what your sarcasm does to me, Miss Blackwood." His voice was sultry, and I was glad I was alone, so no one could see the way my thighs clenched as my body betrayed me.

"What do you want?" My voice slightly shaky.

"I need you to put on that black dress you wore that first night I saw you in the club."

"Why?"

"Well, I think the pleasure of seeing you in that dress was short-lived. And I didn't include you in my plans with Alexei and that is a mistake I do not intend to make again. I don't know much about the second man on your list. I know that he calls himself the Spider and all of his men are Hunters." I rolled my eyes and ignored the comment, but I realized that's what Emery must have meant when she said she was attacked by 'his hunters'.

"A Mercenary solely hunting other Mercenaries? That's a little sadistic."

"And a member of The Spiral. Another reason I don't want you stumbling upon him yourself," he admitted. "And before you argue, yes I know this will involve violence but that does not mean I can't worry about you and the shit you get yourself into."

"I mean are you sure you can handle it? I get myself into a lot of shit. It's a full-time job and last I heard you were retired."

This time he laughed but brushed over it.

"Some things I am willing to come out of retirement for. Anyway, The Spider is holding a party at a mansion downtown and it seems he heard about our little... meeting last night. I got an invitation this morning and it says to bring a plus one."

"You aren't going to bring Avery?" I hated how pathetic that made me sound.

"Like I said, I'm not going to try and leave you out again. Besides, we were always the better team." I sat in silence for a moment, thinking about it.

"You mean when you try to boss me around and throw me over your shoulder like a fucking child? I think I work better on my own, thank you."

He laughed, "I gave you the option to walk away, Arabella. You decided not to and I don't make empty threats." I rolled my eyes.

"And if I decided to go on my own?" He let out a low growl that sent a panic through me that I wasn't sure how to take.

"Try it." There was so much violence behind those two words and even though he wasn't here, I could feel the promise he held behind them.

"Fine," I replied, my voice shaky. "But I'm going to finish my food first and think of all of the things I want to do to hurt you in my head." This time he laughed, a low sexy chuckle.

"I could think of a few things that you could do to me that we'd both enjoy, Arabella." A small squeak involuntarily left my lungs as heat flooded my cheeks. Fuck, this man was going to take what little resolve I had left in me.

"Goodbye, Keiran." I didn't wait for a reply before I hung up. And I don't think that the color ever left my face as I finished my food before getting ready. I dressed exactly as I had that first night after running into Keiran, though this time, I strapped the dagger to my inner thigh in case I needed it. He met me in the front yard sometime later and his eyes glazed over my whole body, lingering at my thighs. I watched him rub his thumb along his full bottom lip and his earlier words filled my head again. "Is it too much? Maybe I should change. The cocktail dress was a terrible idea during a fight, but it was the only one that covered the Bind. Which, should I really be walking around with this thing showing on my arm?"

At this point, I was just babbling, speaking nonsense until I looked back up at him. He stepped right in front of me and instinctively I tried to take a step back. But he grabbed me, and I watched as his Aura slipped through his fingertips and encircled my arm. A strange soothing feeling encased the burns, and I watched as they started to dissipate and completely disappear.

"Unfortunately, I can't remove the actual Bind. But I can remove the burns. I was going to last night, but you were quite angry with me."

"I was quite angry with everybody last night," I admitted. "Not to mention, being carried out with my ass in the air over your shoulder kind of took the fun out of everything." His smile was wicked.

"No, you shouldn't change," he said, answering my earlier question before he looked me up and down again. I sighed, realizing how long a year without sex really was.

"You have to stop looking at me like that," I said, pushing around him to walk toward the car. And to hide my facial expressions.

"Like what?" He was quicker than me as he opened the door for me.

"Like you want to devour me. It makes my brain malfunction." I watched him knit his eyebrows together before closing the door behind me and getting into the driver's side.

"I've always found you attractive, Arabella." I've always heard him say that. Even before we were told that one of us had to marry one of the Stark brothers, Keiran would flirt with me like his life depended on it. But he never crossed the line, never took it too far despite him fucking anything that would move. So, I never really believed it. I just took it at face value even if I desperately wanted it to be true. I rolled my eyes.

"You think every woman that graces your presence is attractive. That's not saying much."

"I hate when you do that," he replied, his tone annoyed as he pulled out of my mother's driveway.

"Do what?"

"Try and make yourself seem less than you are. You can't lump yourself in with everyone else, Arabella because there is no fucking comparison." His eyes passed back and forth between me and the road, a mix of frustration, pain, and guilt swirling around in those dangerous eyes.

"And I hate when you do that," I said after a moment. He knit his eyebrows together in confusion.

"What are you talking about?"

"Say shit like that because it makes the hatred I have for you chip away that much more. I've worked hard to build this wall around my little black heart, Keiran." My tone was lighthearted, trying to hide the fact that I was uncomfortable with how personal the conversation was going. He smiled again, though I could still sense the tension between us.

We sat silently for the rest of the drive which I was more than okay with. But as he pulled the car up to a large golden gate that separated the house from the rest of the world, he turned to me, gently grabbing my chin to look at him. I flinched, the memory of Alexander doing the same the day before, though much more violent, replaying in my head. And I saw anger flash in his eyes again, the same kind of anger that rolled off of him in waves when he saw the burns yesterday. But his fingers were ever so gentle as he looked me in my eyes.

"I'm gonna break that wall, baby girl. Whether you like it or not, and I'm going to make you see just how beautiful you really are." My cheeks heated again as he pulled away from me just in time for the golden gate to swing open. As we continued inside, his smile turned devious again. "Besides, what kind of man would I be if I didn't tell my future wife she was beautiful?" I scoffed loudly.

"We're not engaged."

"Not yet," he laughed. "But it's gonna happen, baby. I told you; you still owe me a wedding." I rolled my eyes again.

"Keep dreaming, pal."

"Oh, I do. Every night," he laughed. I sighed again as he drove down the long driveway lined with vibrant green moss-covered trees. The place was huge with a large property that seemed to have no end in the darkness. The gravel was lit by twinkling white lights that led to a bustling mansion. Fancy cars wrapped around the driveway as people handed their keys to the valets and made their way inside. I looked around in awe, completely unaware that Keiran had already gotten out and was opening my door. I sat for a moment, a pit growing in my stomach because I had no idea what I was walking into. Sensing my unease, he ducked down to meet my gaze before reaching his hand out for mine.

"It's going to be okay," he said, his tone serious and I wanted so badly to believe him. I took a slow, deep breath, and with a slight tinge from the bruising in my ribs, I was made painfully aware that I had no choice.

With a sigh, I took his hand and found myself pressing further into his side as we made our way into the place. I don't know why but every fiber of my being was screaming that I did not want to be there. He was starting to pick up on my panic as he let go of my hand, just long enough to hand an invitation to a masked man, half naked and painted in gold like a statue, standing at the entrance. I hadn't realized that I was frozen in place until Keiran was behind me, his arm around my waist as he bent down to whisper in my ear.

"Relax, Arabella. I will not let them hurt you." I turned to face him, not even bothering trying to get away from him this time and met that intense stare. "I promise." Whether I believed him or not, I knew I needed to do this. With another slow, deep breath, I nodded and allowed him to lead me further inside. This time his arm stayed tight around my waist, which only calmed me for a moment until that sickly sweet, slightly decaying scent filled my nose.

Inside the mansion was even more breathtaking than the outside. The entrance led into a giant foyer and beyond that a grand double-sided staircase that opened to a large balcony overlooking everyone. Beautifully dressed party goers were scattered throughout the place in various forms of intoxication and gold painted men and women intricately danced among them to a strange, yet alluring music that filled the air.

But there, scattered throughout them, were over a dozen Necros. Though to the untrained eye they looked like nothing more than sickly humans, the scent of their rotten decaying insides invaded my senses. Their skin, almost translucent and paper thin, pulled tightly over their jagged crooked bones and their fingertips blackened by the blood caked underneath their nail beds. Should one of them smile you'd be able to smell the rotted flesh between their sharpened teeth and despite having smelt it many times before, it still turned my insides. I stiffened again in Keiran's embrace as another painted patron met us with a tray of drinks.

"Would you like a glass of wine?" The woman asked, her high-pitched voice rather excited. He held up his free hand, probably realizing the same thing I had in that moment. It was most likely whatever was in that drink that made everyone unaware of the creatures around them.

"No thank you," Kieran offered and I could hear the disgust in his voice. "Will the host be making an appearance tonight?" She looked rather defeated that he didn't take her offer but smiled at the mention of her boss.

"Of course. He is actually just up there." I followed her extended hand as she motioned toward the staircase and there, I saw him. His hair slicked back and painted the same metallic red that adorned his toned bare chest, and he wore a red glass devil mask unlike the gold and black lace of those he provided for the staff, giving no ideas as to what he really looked like. He stood with his arms extended out, resting on the balcony as he looked down on those beneath him. As if he could feel us staring, his gaze snapped toward us and landed on me. I felt that panic rising in me again and every ounce of my being knew this man was dangerous. I tensed up, ready to turn around and leave when Alexander's voice sounded from in front of us.

"As breathtaking as ever, Miss Blackwood." Before I could respond, Keiran pushed me back, placing himself between the two of us.

"What the fuck are you doing here, Alexander?" There was venom in Keiran's tone, and I flinched at the intensity in his eyes. Alexander smiled viciously, ignoring him as he continued.

"Perhaps we shall have a dance together."

"If you lay a hand on her, I'll break every one of your fucking fingers."

"Hmm," he taunted. "But I already have. How do you think she got that Bind in the first place." As if I had electrocuted him with my touch, Keiran pulled away from me, snapping around to look me in the eyes.

"He is the one that bound you?" There was fury I had never seen before in his eyes. It scared me more than I wanted to admit. "You're working for my fucking father?" By this time some of the others had taken notice of the commotion going on. Several of the Necros had also taken notice, inching their way closer to us, making all the hairs on the back of my neck stand up. If we were going to have to fight, I needed to be ready.

"Your father?" I asked, my legs subtly shifting to a fighting stance as I held my arms at my side. "Keiran, I- I didn't know."

"It was a fact I didn't disclose," Alexander responded, his tone still humorous. "I suppose you can't pin all the blame on her." He lifted his shoulders as if to shrug off his guilt. Keiran stepped closer to him, the anger pulsating from him like electric shock currents and acted as if he didn't notice them circling us like vultures.

"Keiran, please." I reached for him, but he recoiled from my touch, sending a pang of guilt through me.

"Don't touch me," he snapped.

"I am surprised that you managed to remove the burn from her arm," Alexander chuckled, his condescending tone forcing its way through the tension. "Perhaps next time she disobeys I shall carve it into her flesh instead." I watched all the resolve leave Keiran as he lunged for him. I raised both hands, my intention to step between them, with force if I had to. I was stopped, however, as the man in the devil mask had the same idea, his large form pushing between them to rest his hands on both of their chests. I snuck a glance at Keiran, the veins in his neck protruding with so much anger.

"Gentleman," he said, his voice strange. Almost as if he were changing it to further his disguise. "You are disturbing my other guests."

CHAPTER FIFTEEN

Keiran

All I could see was red. I could feel the Necros growing anxious around us, feeding on the anger that was spewing from me. But the thought of Alexander being anywhere near me let alone Arabella, had pushed me past my breaking point. As he reached for her, as if he fucking owned her, all my resolve had dissolved, and I lunged for his throat. I was going to fucking kill him.

"Gentlemen." I had been so angry that I hadn't noticed him step between us, placing his hand on both of us to hold us back from tearing at each other's throats. "You are disturbing my other guests." I could feel my Aura encircling me, building the more Alexander smirked at me. If I didn't take a step back, I was going to reach a point that I didn't want to. "Surely, we can settle this like civilized-"

"I'm going to remove your fucking head for hurting her," I said, cutting him off before turning to leave. I slipped my arm around Arabella's waist again. I was so furious with her, but I needed to get us out of here. I needed to get away from Alexander before blood was spilled in front of those disgusting creatures.

As sickly as they seemed, Necros were extremely powerful. Unhindered by the qualms of being a living being, they had no care for how or why they fought. Their only objective was the kill, and they'd achieve it anyway necessary and neither of us were prepared for a fight of that magnitude. Not to mention if the one who had called them here, I'm assuming The Spider himself, was hoping for a fight, we would be completely blindsided. So for now, we had to retreat.

"Just remember Arabella, until you pay me what you owe or until this job is complete, you will be bound to me." Alexander's irritating voice crawled over the suffocating tension in the room. I clenched my jaw and pulled her away with me until we were outside. I let go of her, the contact between us too much. She stumbled after me though she kept quiet as we got into the car, and I sped away so fast that the tires threw rocks. I don't know how long it had been before she finally spoke.

"I didn't know that he was your father." Her voice was quiet. "I knew so little about him because you never spoke of it."

"You have your unresolved trauma. Well, my father is mine." I could feel her studying my face, but I didn't look at her. Just kept my expression stoic as I kept my eyes on the road. She grew quiet again, no doubt lost in thought.

"Why do you think he had them there? Do you think his plan was to kill us all along?" I looked at her again but ignored her question.

"How much did you steal from him?" She bit down on her lip, her eyebrows knit together as if she didn't want to answer.

"I've paid off half by the jobs I've done for him already."

"How much?" She was avoiding the question.

"I still owe him 5."

"Million?" She said nothing, giving me my answer.

"What were you thinking, Arabella?" She sighed.

"That I needed to survive," she admitted.

"By running away? You had a whole life here. A family. You fucking had me."

"Right. A fucking family. What a joke." Her tone had grown angry. "I was always treated like I didn't belong. I was never good enough in any one of their eyes, including yours, and that night just made me realize what I didn't want to see the whole time." By now we had reached Jezebel's house and thank the gods for that because I threw the car into park rather harshly before turning back toward her.

"Are you fucking kidding me? I'd have given every fucking thing I had to you." She rolled her eyes, exasperated.

"Right. I could tell when you were buried in Avery on our living room sofa how much you thought of me." I clenched my jaw.

"It was a mistake!" My voice was louder than I had intended. "I had just found out that the woman I loved was destined to-" Fuck. I was so angry the words slipped out before I could stop myself and I knew she picked up on it, by the way her eyes shot up. I shook my head, turning away from her again. "Just get out."

"Keiran-"

"Now, Arabella." She wanted to protest, and I could feel her anger, feel her Aura growing more intense by the second. But I couldn't explain it to her. Not yet. Not until I could break the Bind between her and Alexander and make sure that she was safe. She slammed the door and didn't look back as she went inside. I sped away toward my place, my mind going a thousand miles an hour as I dialed Avery's number.

"Well, that was fast. Did you get any information on the Spider?"

Ignoring her question, I said, "I need you to meet me at

the penthouse. And bring an empty duffel bag." I didn't wait for her response as I hung up and tossed the phone onto my passenger seat.

When I pulled into the apartment building, I sped up to the top parking floor and pulled into the space quickly before heading inside. Avery wasn't here yet, so I used these couple minutes of quiet to allow my thoughts to overtake me. 5 million was a lot of money. I had more than enough stashed away to cover it. But the thought of what she had to do to get it was enough to drive me insane.

I grabbed a decanter and a glass from the bar to pour myself a drink. I loosened the tie around my neck and rolled my sleeves up before taking a seat on my dark gray sofa. I took a swig and leaned my head back, allowing my eyes to roll shut. Fuck I was tired.

I heard the door open before I looked up to see Avery with the bag in one hand and the other resting on her hip, that same glare that she always had resting on her face. I set my glass down on the table and stood up with a groan before walking over to an original piece hanging on my wall. I slid my finger across the bottom of the frame, popping open the hidden safe built into the stone tile below it and quickly typed in the 6-digit code that unlocked it. I reached for the bag.

"That bad of a night huh?" She asked. Placing the bag beside me, I knelt and gathered a couple stacks of the money I had hidden away, tucking them neatly into the bag before locking the safe back up. I sighed.

"Arabella's boss is my father." Avery's eyes grew large, and her mouth nearly popped open with shock.

"How did you find that out?" I grabbed my drink from the table.

"He showed up tonight. Practically rubbed it in my face." I downed the remaining alcohol before filling it again and taking my place on the sofa once more. Avery pressed her lips in annoyance as she often did when it came to talking about her sister.

"It doesn't surprise me. She's so reckless."

"Regardless of how you feel about her it has always been our responsibility to make sure her power does not fall into the wrong hands."

"Yes, I know," she snapped. "Doesn't mean that I have to like her. I fucking hate her, Keiran." I shot her an angry glance.

"Watch it," I warned her. She rolled her eyes.

"Don't worry, Keiran. I am aware that she is the love of your life." Her tone was mocking. She fell back into the other end of the sofa, her arms crossed defensively over her chest. "You haven't let me forget it since that night." I leaned forward with one arm resting on my knee and the other pinching the bridge of my nose.

That had been a long night. Jezebel had just told us about what the seer had shown her in a vision and all of us were on edge. No one had uttered a word about the Condemned apart from whispered stories we told children to keep them in line. And now suddenly they were a potential threat that we never saw coming, and it put Arabella in even more danger than she already had been.

As if her burden wasn't big enough already. A burden she wasn't even aware of. She and I had already been fighting that night because I had stupidly tried to distance myself from her like Jezebel had asked. And now I was going to have to distance myself while also watching her every move to make sure he couldn't find her if he ever did show up? It was damn near impossible. So instead, I tried to drown my problems in a bottle of jack and wound up making the biggest mistake of my life. I couldn't even remember the act itself, but I will never forget the sobering look on Arabella's face when she came through the front door and found the two of us together. And I'd never forgive myself for what happened after she left...

"If Alexander were to ever find out the truth, it would affect us all," I muttered, pulling myself back to the present. "We created this problem and now I'm going to fix it."

CHAPTER SIXTEEN

Arabella

I should have been focused on the Spider and why he had us surrounded the moment we entered the mansion. I had a sneaking suspicion that his involvement had something to do with the reason why there hadn't been a single Necro attack since I arrived back here. But instead, all night I mulled over what Keiran had said. Or really, what he hadn't said. I refused to hold on to his words about the woman he had been in love with. But the bit about finding out what she had been destined for kept replaying over and over to the point that I couldn't sleep. That comment, coupled with what my mother had said, told me exactly what I already knew. They were lying to me and keeping me at arm's length as they always had.

As light began to cascade through my window, I had worked myself up quite a bit. I was frustrated and I needed answers. I grabbed my phone from the nightstand and sent a text to Keiran.

ME: I find it awfully hypocritical of you to be angry about Alexander when you are hiding something from me too. I tossed the phone down next to me as my mind was racing, the anger bubbling up in me the more I thought about it.

ME: I never intentionally withheld that he was your father because I didn't even know. But you have dodged discussing why you know so much about the amulet every time it is brought up. I was thinking through my next text when my phone buzzed with his reply.

HIM: I can see you are angry with me. But this is not a conversation that should be had over text. What a fucking asshole I said aloud as I quickly replied again.

ME: Don't patronize me. You are lying to me and pushing me away just as much as I ever did. Either you have the amulet, or you know who does and all of you have done nothing but gaslight me to appease you of your own guilt. Within maybe five seconds of sending the last text, my phone started ringing. It was Keiran but I was so pissed off that I ignored it and left it on the bed. I made my way to the kitchen, seeking my only life source at this point. I was so preoccupied with mentally cussing him out that by the time I saw Avery, I was already bumping into her.

"Watch where you are going," she sneered. I rolled my eyes, stepping around her and started making a pot of coffee. "Are you just going to act like I'm not here?"

I scoffed, "Don't act like you'd be offended if I didn't speak to you, Avery. You want to avoid me just as much as I want to avoid you." She spun around to face me, her lips pressed together in annoyance.

"That may be so but unfortunately, you are the reason I am here." She reached behind her to grab a dark blue bag that I hadn't noticed from the table and pushed it toward me. "He wants you to use this to break the bind." Curious, I unzipped the bag, and my eyes nearly popped out of my head. "He said it's more than what you owe." I shook my head.

"There is no way I can take that much money from him."

She rolled her eyes, crossing her arms over her chest.

"You have no idea how dangerous Alexander really is, Arabella. Since you were stupid enough to get yourself added to his roster, he now has to fix it." She was really starting to piss me off too.

"Fuck you, Avery," I replied. "You've always acted like you were better than me."

"Because I hate you." I lifted an eyebrow, almost amused.

"At least we are being honest now."

"I hate that everything was always about you," she continued, her tone mocking. I scoffed.

"You were the golden child, Avery. Everything you did was fucking perfect in everyone else's eyes and you never let me forget it."

"Because I fucking despised you from the moment I understood what that meant. I wanted to take everything from you just because I could. Including Keiran but you've always had your claws so deep in him that that was a wasted effort." A sadistic grin creeped across her face. "Although, I don't think he thought about you at all while he was fucking me." Before I could stop myself, I punched Avery in the face and she stumbled back, bringing her hand up to her bleeding lip. I expected her to swing back but instead she laughed. "I even envy the amount of fight you have in you." She shook her head, wiping away the blood on the sleeve of her blue sweater. "This is your only way out. Just take it for what it is." She said nothing else as she left me standing there.

After her little revelation, I avoided everyone for the rest of the day. I had sent a message to Alexander that I needed to meet him somewhere that night and after he responded that he'd only meet with me at Keiran's club, I shut my phone off. But holding this much money was making me uneasy. All I could think about was the night that I met Alexander.

When I knew that Damian was going to kill me, I was aware that my only option was to kill him instead. While fighting to stay conscious under the weight of his hands, I barely managed to drag my hands up to his face. I dug my fingernails into his cheek, and he let go of me for just a moment, but it was all I needed.

"Fucking cunt," he spit through gritted teeth and tried to grab me again. Encasing them in my Aura, I slammed my palms against his chest and just like Keiran had taught me, I pushed it into his flesh like sharpened tendrils. I felt it pierce his heart and he stumbled back, clutching at his chest as blood coated his mouth. His face had become so grotesque, and I watched as he realized he was dying. He grabbed at me again, ripping the shirt that I wore and getting his blood all over my arms and face. I felt the icy feeling shoot through my veins and as he dropped to the ground, lifeless, I panicked.

I didn't even know if anyone had seen me, but I took off running. I think I ran until the sun started to come up and that's when I had concocted my plan that I was going to disappear. I was so angry with Keiran, but I knew that he wouldn't forgive me. Not for this. I was crying by the time I stumbled across an unlocked car parked outside of an old building that looked like it had been abandoned. I searched it in a hurry and by some Divine intervention, in the glove box I found a black diamond necklace. I knew it was a rarity because the diamond only turned black when it was infused. Whoever had owned it was going to be pissed but I also knew what it would go for on the black market.

And after a quick call to an illegal seller, it was only a matter of minutes before there was a potential buyer. Within an hour, I had sold the necklace for a small fraction of what it was really worth and was on a train heading for the furthest destination I could find. Over the next few weeks, I dispersed the money between several prepaid cards so that if anyone came looking, I'd have no trail. Or so I thought.

I had settled in a quiet little beach town, void of any supernatural being so I thought I was safe. Unfortunately, Alexander was better as he had followed me from the moment I had sold the necklace because I hadn't known that the person I stole it from had actually already sold it to him. They were supposed to deliver it that night, but I had gotten to it first. One night when I returned to the small apartment I had managed to get for myself, I was met with Alexander holding a knife to my neck telling me I owed him my life for what I had taken from him. 10 million dollars. That's what my life had been worth.

• •

CHAPTER SEVENTEEN

Keiran

I knew she was angry and despite Avery and Jezebel warning me against it, I was going to tell her the truth. All of it if it meant that she wouldn't disappear again. But she ignored my calls for the rest of the day. Avery had told me about their conversation, so I understood why she didn't want to talk.

But as I stood on the balcony of the club, I noticed her moving through the crowd of people. The blue duffel bag was clinging to her chest, and I could tell she was nervous as she made her way to the VIP booths. When she reached the second floor, she scanned the area until her eyes met mine. She froze for a moment before trying to seem indifferent as she sat down at one of the booths.

"What are you doing here?" I asked her. She bit down on her lip and averted her eyes from me.

"This was the only place he would meet me," she replied, and I could see the guilt in her face. The rage I suddenly felt must have been evident on my face as she tried to shrink down into the leather seat. "Keiran, I-"

"I just wanted to see what the hype was about." Alexander's voice was like nails on a chalkboard as he slid into the booth next to her, sliding his arm around the back of her. I had already resolved that I was going to break his fucking fingers as soon as I got the chance. And the disgust for this man that painted her face as she put distance between them, solidified it. "And she's the one who said she wanted to meet me." Back was that arrogant smugness as I was physically fighting the urge to bash his face in.

"Here." Her voice had more force behind it as she slid the bag over to him.

"Oh? What's this?" He grabbed the bag, curiosity getting the better of him as he gripped it. Unzipping it quickly, he glanced down at its contents before lifting an eyebrow and looking back at me in amusement.

"It's more than what she owes you." My tone was filled with hatred. "Think of it as payment to get the fuck out of here." He sat quietly for a moment before turning to Arabella.

"Was I such a terrible boss that you would be in debt to another just to get rid of me?" She knit her eyebrows together as if she had suddenly realized something but chose not to say it.

"The worst," she replied, her face stoic. I wanted to laugh. I loved her fucking sarcasm. She held her arm out toward him. "Now break it." He leaned back in the booth again, his lips pressed in dissatisfaction. I knew that face all too well. It was the face he made when things didn't turn out the way he wanted them too. It usually was followed by him beating the fuck out of me or Damian. Instinctively, I moved toward Arabella, ready to defend her from his movements. He laughed and viciously grabbed her arm.

"Relax, boy," he replied with a grin. "How am I supposed to remove it if I can't touch her?" I said nothing, only watched him intensely as he continued. His free hand hovered above where her Bind was hidden, and she watched quietly as his Aura spilled from his open palm like a thick black tar. It encased her forearm, making the Bind visible once again and she jolted upright. He pulled his palm back, pulling with it the contents of the Bind out of her skin, like pulling the ink off of a page. I watched her face twist in pain, though she bit down on her lip to keep from crying out. "I have to admit, Arabella. I'm quite disappointed that you'll no longer be working for me. You really were quite good at doing my bidding." The last remnants of the black magick slid from her arm, leaving a bleeding wound behind it and she pulled it back to cradle it against her chest.

"Let me heal it." I kept my eyes on Alexander as I held out my hand toward her. She hesitated but held it out for me. Gently, my Aura encircled her arm as it had with the burns and despite her trying to hide it, I heard her whimper from the pain. He watched with a smile on his face.

"You really do enjoy this," Arabella said with such disgust, but he only laughed before he stood up from the booth.

"You forget that you've spent the last 5 years with me, Arabella. I know you better than he does. And despite what you want everyone to believe, you enjoyed the power you felt not having them holding you back. Telling you that you aren't good enough." He began to walk away, calling over his shoulder but I watched the hurt cross her face, the disgrace when she realized that he was right. "You're only going to hold her back, Keiran. If you don't realize that quickly enough, she is going to be the death of you."

CHAPTER EIGHTEEN

Arabella

The stinging in my arm was beginning to fade as Alexander disappeared down into the crowd of people. But it didn't matter. I was finally free of my ties to that man and everything that came along with it. All of the time I spent trying to be good enough at what I did so that he wouldn't change his mind and take my life. All of the dangerous situations I had gotten myself into trying to prove something, now simple moments of my past.

"I don't trust him." Keiran's voice brought me back from my reverie, but I couldn't help the guilt that flooded my face when I looked at him. I had only spent a minute fraction of my time with that man, and it was enough to give me nightmares. He had spent his entire childhood enduring the consequences of Alexander's whims and frustrations and I could see the strain he hid behind that blue gaze. The strain that I had also added to. It was a wonder how he didn't end up like his brother. "How do we know he actually broke the Bind?"

"He did," I replied. "I can't feel it anymore." I could still feel the anger emitting from his body as he finally turned from the direction he had gone, to look at me. I could tell there was so much that he wanted to say. So much that needed to be said between us. "Can I tell you something?"

"What?" His voice was tired.

"He's not wrong," I admitted. "About how I felt." I searched his face for a reaction but there was nothing, just that stoic stare. It made me uncomfortable, and I darted my eyes to the glossy black table in front of me. "That night, Keiran-"

"We don't have to talk about it," he said, cutting me off. I shook my head, this time forcing myself to meet his gaze.

"Yes, we do." I paused for a moment, trying to gather my thoughts. "Damian nearly killed me and for a moment, I was going to let him." I watched him wince, trying to hide the agony of my words. "I felt so worthless in that moment that I was going to just let him take my life. But then the thought of being vulnerable to another living being again, of doubting my worth again because the actions of other people, made me so fucking angry." I could feel the tears stinging the back of my eyes and I had to blink them back before he could notice. "I wanted him to feel every ounce of fear, every fiber of hatred that I had inside of me. I enjoyed it and I killed him because he deserved it."

"Do you think that it will make me see you differently?" he asked. I shook my head.

"No," I admitted. "I just want you to understand that despite the fact that I hate him, I never would have accepted the way that I felt that night unless Alexander allowed me to do so." His arms were now crossed over his chest, and I watched him clench his jaw in anger.

"I never would have made you feel guilty."

"I didn't run because I felt guilty. I ran because I was afraid of you."

"Do you honestly think that I would have held his life above yours? That I would have gone after you because you killed the man that tried to kill you?" His voice was higher, angrier now. "Is that honestly what you think of me? That I'm just a monster like the two of them?" Now he wasn't even hiding the hurt in his face, and I felt a ball of emotion forming in my chest.

"Keiran-"

"You have no idea what I felt, Arabella. You have no fucking clue what I have done to get to you, what I have given up to bring you back. And for what? For you to compare me to one of them?"

"I'm not comparing you." My voice sounded small, nearly drowned out by the melodic techno song playing in the background.

"I can't-" He shook his head, stumbling over his words like the realization hit him like a freight train. "I can't do this anymore, Arabella."

"What does that mean?" I felt a sudden panic rising in my chest, like the collar of my hoodie was tightening as he spoke.

"This." He moved his hand between the two of us. "I can't keep trying to fix this when its clear that you don't want to." He spoke over his shoulder as he too started to walk away in the same direction Alexander had gone. "If you truly see me in the same light as them, then there is nothing here anymore. I'm sorry it took me so long to figure that out."

"Wait!" I hadn't realized the desperation I felt at that moment. Was this what he felt every time I walked away from him? I should have asked him to stay. I should have told him that it wasn't that I saw him in the same light as Alexander, or Damian, or my father. That was the problem. He was leagues above them and despite how much he wanted me to believe otherwise, I was never going to see myself as good enough for him because of it. And despite that, I was selfish and the thought of losing him was eating away at me.

But of course, that fear of vulnerability was raising its ugly head. And the one thing that I recoiled from more than close proximity was being honest with someone that I cared about. He stopped but refused to look back at me.

"Am I now in your debt for breaking the Bind?" It was such a shitty thing to say, I know. And I felt my heart break the moment it left my lips.

"Fuck you, Arabella."

****

I don't even know when I ended up at the bar. I couldn't even decipher how much time had passed between the man doused in axe body spray offering to buy me a drink, and the room starting to spin. I vaguely remembered that I had to count the number of drinks I had on both hands, and another being poured as I drunkenly leaned against the bar counter. Sakura's gaze would find its way toward me every so often as she attended guests on the other end of the bar, but her coworker paid it no mind as long as I was making him money. Axe body spray snaked his arm around my waist, trying to be seductive as his hot breath hit my ear.

"You want to get out of here?" he asked, his words slurred. I rolled my eyes.

"No," I replied bluntly. "I've had my fair share of disappointment lately. I really don't want another 2 minutes of it with you." I pushed away from him and downed the shot that the bartender had placed in front of me, before stumbling my way onto the dance floor. The song had transitioned into something seductive with a lot of bass and another patron dressed in leather who smelled strongly of cigarettes and vanilla, was behind me. His rough hands slid under the fabric of my hoodie and settled on my waist, our bodies swaying in rhythm with the music. I closed my eyes, enjoying the way we melded together, enjoying the warmth of his hands on my skin. A barefoot woman with ebony skin and alluring dark eyes dressed in a white lace crop top and mini skirt joined us, pinning me between the 2 of them but I didn't care. At least not at that moment. Anything to stop the storm thrashing around inside my head. They kept me there, pulling me along with them into the next song. I tried to stay in rhythm, tried to focus on the way my body felt but was distracted by a constant sound that didn't seem to fit quite right with the rest of the song. A repetitive beat that was growing louder by the second.

"Are you okay?" The woman asked, her beautiful, toned body still swaying to a song I could no longer hear.

"You don't hear that?"

"The song?"

"No. That beating sound."

"Did you take something?" The man asked, his mouth at my ear. I shook my head as I pulled out of their embrace.

They didn't follow me as I pushed my way through the rest of the crowd. The air around me was starting to thicken and the space felt like it was boxing me in. I managed to stumble my way outside as my breathing quickened, and I suddenly realized where that sound was coming from. My heartbeat was rising rapidly, the sound of its beating thrumming loudly in my ears as my panic attack started to overtake me.

I leaned forward, placing my hands on my knees as I tried to steady myself, but I couldn't catch my breath. I clawed at my hoodie, ripping it off of me. I took a sharp inhale of breath as the cool night breeze outside brushed against the skin exposed beneath my crop top. It didn't help however, as I started to hyperventilate. I leaned back against the cold stone wall. I dropped my head in my hands, the quick repetitive breaths doing nothing to help as my vision started to blur. If I couldn't get it under control, I was going to pass out.

All of the sounds around me intensified and I could vaguely hear someone speaking but I couldn't focus. All I could think about was what I had just done. How I pushed the one person that I still held close to me regardless of how hard I tried, away for the last time. I had pushed Keiran away because I was too fucking selfish to notice what my actions had done. I just needed Keiran to know that I didn't mean it! That I didn't want to lose him.

"Please, don't leave me," I pleaded before passing out.

CHAPTER NINETEEN

Keiran

I don't know why I expected to get any work done. One of my jobs as Proctor of this city was to work out negotiations and deals. Some arguing prices on contracts between Mercenaries and whoever hired them, others negotiating assignments for the Spiral. I was very good at what I did, very good at staying levelheaded but with her, all my resolve went out the door. I meant most of what I said. It killed me that she saw me in the same light as my family and I couldn't keep fighting for something if it wasn't reciprocated. There would never be any compromise, never any negotiation. Only heartbreak.

"Fuck," I said, frustrated as I dropped my hands down on my desk with a loud thud. I was always going to want her, regardless of how hard I could try not to.

My phone pinged from inside my pocket, nearly the tenth time within the last 30 minutes. I was trying to ignore it, trying to wallow in my self-pity for just a moment longer but it was starting to irritate me. With a sigh, I retrieved it from my pocket and opened it to a slew of messages from Sakura, which was unusual for her. She never texted me when she knew I was working, and especially not when she was on the clock.

At first the messages were just informative, letting me know that there was a man buying Arabella drinks at the bar. I hated the jealousy that surged through me at that, but I kept reading as they seemed to be a bit more frantic as they went on. Sakura thought that the guy was trying to do something to her as he kept paying for shot after shot and Arabella was taking them left and right. He tried taking her home which she turned him down quickly. Her last message read:

Sakura: I think something is wrong. She just ran outside.

I couldn't help the ball forming in my chest. Was Alexander planning something and she figured it out? Against my better judgment, I made my way outside of the club but what I found was almost worse. I found her there, tearing away at her hoodie as if it were restricting her airways before she fell back against the wall, her head in her hands. She was hyperventilating, unable to catch her breath.

"Arabella calm down." I don't think she heard me as she started into a full-blown panic attack.

"I just need Keiran to know that I didn't mean it." I don't think she was aware of anything around her, certainly not that I was crouched in front of her, trying to get her attention. "I need him to know that I don't want to lose him…Please don't leave me." Her voice was so desperate between her gasps for air before she went limp, her body falling forward into my arms.

Grabbing onto her like she'd break if I let go, I rushed her to my car. I gently placed her in the back seat and sent a quick text to Sakura, telling her that everything was okay and that I was leaving with her so there was no longer a need to worry. I jumped in the driver's seat and sped off. I thought about taking her to the hospital, but I knew that would only upset her more. I could already hear her getting angry with herself for allowing it to happen. As if she could control it. I sighed.

"That's your problem you know," I said, though I was aware she couldn't hear me at the moment. "You always have to be in control, and this is what it does to you."

"Hmm." I heard her groan and looked back to see her eyes open, but I could tell she was still barely aware. Not to mention incredibly drunk. I could smell the alcohol coming from her like a strong perfume.

"You had a panic attack and passed out," I said, trying to keep her attention. "I'm going to take you back home." I watched her through the rear-view mirror as she shook her head violently.

"I don't want to go back there."

"Why not?"

"I don't want to see Avery and her stupid face." I couldn't help the laugh that escaped me. "Do you know what she said to me?" She managed to sit upright but was clearly still very intoxicated, continuing with a conversation that I think started in her head. "She said- and I quote-" She held up her hands as if to emphasize it. "'I don't think he thought about you at all while he was fucking me'. I mean..." She leaned back, her expression animated. "Who says that?"

"I'll tell you who," she said, answering her own question. "Avery because she hates me."

"No, she doesn't," I offered, side stepping the other comment. We would have to talk about it, but she was going to be sober for that conversation.

"Yes, she does. She told me and I don't even know why. I used to want to be just like her because she always got everything right. She was so perfect and strong." She rolled her eyes. "The whole time she was just wishing I failed. How stupid of me."

"I do hope that you continue to be this honest about how you feel once you sober up."

"I doubt it," she said, which made me laugh again. "Besides it doesn't really matter what I say anymore because I fucked it up. One thing Avery was right about was that I'm reckless and stupid. Hence why I'm drunk in the back of your car." She moved her gaze out the back passenger window, trying unsuccessfully to focus before she leaned her head back against the seat. "I'm really dizzy. How much longer until we are at my hotel? Wait. Did I even tell you to take me there? I think I just thought it but never said it out loud."

"There is a lot to unpack in that whole thing," I said, an amused grin on my face. "One; we're going to discuss everything you just said tomorrow when you are sober. Secondly, no you never told me to take you there, but I wouldn't even if you had. Third; please try not to puke until we get to my place."

"Why are we going to your place?" She kept her head back against the seat, her eyes now shut as she tried to obey my request.

"Because that is the only other safe place for me to take you." She brought her hand up to her forehead, saluting with two fingers.

"Aye, aye captain," she muttered. At least she was a happy drunk. Minus the crippling panic attack that she seems determined not to mention. I was always able to tell when she was upset. Like when her father had pushed her too far or when her sister had struck a nerve in her that she couldn't just brush off. She would usually just walk away, acting like she felt nothing though I could see it in her face. But she had never done that, never had a panic attack like that, and I now wondered if it was a reoccurring thing. The way she suddenly flips when something happens, when a memory is brought up. Did she keep running from me because she didn't want me to know what it was doing to her? How she couldn't just brush it off anymore.

The rest of the car ride was quiet until I parked the car anyway. I tried to help her out of the back seat, which unsurprisingly she refused and managed to crawl her way out. She stumbled forward, barely catching her balance by grabbing onto the sleeve of my shirt. She was determined but I was just as hardheaded as I picked her up, bridal style and walked her inside. She tried to fight, not very well I might add, but gave up halfway through when she couldn't wiggle her way out of my arms. Once I sat her down inside though, she pushed away from me and leaned against the couch for support. She looked around, her gaze still slightly uneasy.

"Of course you live here." She rolled her eyes.

"Is that a bad thing?"

"It just annoys me that everything about you has to be so sexy."

"I'm going to take that as a compliment. Now sit down so I can get you some water and something to eat to soak up the alcohol before you go to bed." She sighed dramatically but plopped down on the couch and sat quietly as I made my way into the kitchen. I grabbed a bottle of water from the fridge and some Tylenol from a hallway cabinet and handed them to her. "Take those." She did as I said without argument, so I went back into the kitchen. I didn't really have much to cook but I did find some leftover lasagna in the fridge which I didn't even bother warming up because I knew she'd like just the way it was. In fact, it made me laugh because it reminded me of the conversation we had. I plated it and grabbed a fork before heading back into the living room. She sat with her arms crossed over her chest, clearly worked up about something, anger on her flushed face.

"Did you call her?" She said, her tone annoyed. I knit my eyebrows together as I handed her the plate. Her eyes lit up, the irritation leaving her for just a moment when she realized it was her favorite.

"Call who?" I watched her take a bite, a small sound of satisfaction leaving her lips before she answered me. I grinned slightly.

"Lacey." The way she said her name was mocking.

"Lacey who?" She took another bite.

"That girl from the diner. She wanted you to call her." As she said it, I looked down and saw the receipt from that day crumbled up on the glass coffee table. I shook my head.

"No."

"Are you going to?" I lifted my eyebrow.

"Are you jealous, Arabella?" This time she blushed, though she tried to hide it by looking down at her food.

"No." Her words sounded forced. "I just- I was just curious." This time I stepped in front of her, placing my finger under her chin so that she had to look up at me. She bit her lip. Fuck I wish I could taste that lip...

"Finish your food so that you can go to bed." I wanted to say so much more. I wanted to tell her that she didn't ruin anything. That I would spend every moment I could trying to prove to her that there would never be anyone except her. But I couldn't. Not until she knew everything. I could see the disappointment in her eyes, like she was expecting me to do something else. She pulled away from me and I had to put some distance between us as I watched her take a couple bites more of her food. She tried to get up to take her plate to the kitchen but instead I grabbed it from her. "No. You sit." She rolled her eyes again, mocking me under her breath as I disappeared into the kitchen. I washed and put away the dishes and grabbed another bottle of water from the fridge before going back. I found her sprawled out across the couch, her hoodie balled up underneath her head like a makeshift pillow. "What the fuck are you doing?"

"You yelled at me to go to bed so that's what I'm trying to do before you so rudely interrupted me." I shook my head and bent down to scoop her up again, tossing her over my shoulder like I had in the club. "What are you doing?" She tried to push off of me, but I slapped her ass and tightened my arms around her legs as I walked with her down the hallway to the bedroom. A squeak escaped her lips, and I knew her cheeks were flushed that pretty little shade of red that they get when she gets excited. She huffed as I sat her down on the bed and disappeared into the closet.

"I'm not a child," she pouted as I returned, tossing her a t-shirt and pointing at the bathroom door that connected to the room.

"Go change and then you can sleep in the bed." She lifted an eyebrow.

"With you?" Perhaps it was just wishful thinking, but her voice sounded hopeful. I shook my head.

"No. I can't sleep next to you."

"Why not?" I made a face.

"Do you really have to ask that, Arabella?" I met her gaze. "There is just too much between us. I cannot confidently say that I would be able to control myself." She rolled her eyes and snatched the t-shirt off of the bed.

"We're both adults. Even if anything were to happen, it's just sex." She pushed past me to get to the bathroom, but I grabbed her arm.

"You and I both know that it would be way more than just sex between us." She looked up at me defiantly.

"I guess we'll never know." I pulled her to me, both hands moving to cup her face. My face was inches from hers, close enough that I could feel the warmth from those pretty fucking lips of hers.

"I'd love to fuck the attitude out of you right now." Her eyes shot up, her cheeks flushing that brilliant shade of red. "But you are drunk and there are things that we have to discuss before I can. So, get your ass in there and change and go to fucking bed."

CHAPTER TWENTY

Arabella

My head was pounding, and I hadn't even opened my eyes yet. I curled up into a ball, squeezing them shut in the hopes that it would help. It didn't and as my bladder made me fully aware that I couldn't stay like this forever, I unfurled my limbs and climbed out of the bed with a groan. I temporarily forgot that Keiran had brought me back to his place and as I stumbled toward his bathroom, I couldn't help but notice how much his home resembled him. Though sleek and elegant, the whole place seemed reserved and quiet. His king-sized bed was covered in a black silk set that matched the thick blackout curtains covering the large window opposite them. His dresser and nightstand were the same shade, and the room was dimly lit by an adjustable lamp. There was also a large walk-in closet that part of me wanted to explore.

I fought the urge though as I made my way to the bathroom. I found my clothes scattered across the floor, including my underwear and I flushed a bright shade of red. I hope I didn't do something stupid. There were no signs of vomit, thankfully, but my clothes did reek of alcohol as I folded them and set them on the countertop. I took a quick shower, stealing some of Keiran's expensive smelling products to wash my hair and body, and was thinking of putting my jeans back on and going commando, when a knock at the door startled me.

"I brought you something!" Her voice echoed behind the door. After I finished towel drying myself and throwing back on Keiran's t-shirt, I opened the door to a very giddy looking Emery. She held a pair of sweatpants and a bottle of water in one hand and some pills in the other. "These were left on the nightstand so I'm guessing he wanted you to take them when you woke up." She handed me the water and pills. "And I figured these would be more comfortable. Although, I don't think he'd mind you walking around like that." She giggled at the embarrassment on my face.

"I feel like a fucking idiot," I groaned as I took the pants from her and slid them on before throwing back the medication with a big gulp of water. She pressed her lips and rolled her eyes.

"You shouldn't. You guys have some shit to work out so it's going to be uncomfortable for a minute. The fact that you are here at all, is all that he cares about."

"I know that's the problem."

"How so?" She leaned against the door frame as if to keep me in here until I admitted how I feel. I stepped around her and made my way back out to the living room.

This part of his apartment seemed even more bare. There was a floor to ceiling window that covered one whole side that looked down on the bustling city below us. A leather sofa sat in the middle of the living space with a glass coffee table and a gorgeous painting of dark green forestry sat high on the wall. There was a granite island counter that divided us from the large kitchen and the floor was made of a dark gorgeous expensive looking tile.

But it was the atmosphere that made the guilt rise in the

back of my throat. It wasn't refined. It was lonely, and I realized this was why he collected those he deemed as strays. He was creating the family that he never had. Filling the void to combat being alone. I could feel his guilt soak every inch of this place and I knew that he had spent every day regretting that night just as much as I had. Maybe even more. I plopped down in the middle of the sofa, a sudden urge to cry clawing at me.

"Because I'm an asshole, Emery." My voice cracked as I spoke, but I held it back. "I never took into consideration what he had been through but the whole time he thought about me."

"You were fighting for your life, Arabella," she offered.

"By making it harder on myself," I admitted. "Keiran was right. I could have come to him right away about what had happened with Alexander, but I still kept it a secret because I'm terrified of being vulnerable with another person. Especially him."

"Well, I could tell you why that is but I kind of was hoping you'd figure it out on your own." I looked at her questioningly. She rolled her eyes, exasperated. "You clearly are still very much in love with each other but are too stubborn to admit it." Before I could even take into consideration what she had said, Keiran walked through the front door, a brown paper bag in his hands. He looked at us both, his eyebrows knit together in confusion.

"When did you get home?" he asked her before closing the door behind him. She jumped up from the couch, running over and capturing him in a hug.

"Just a few minutes ago," she admitted. "I stayed at Sakura's last night and this morning just in case the two of you made up." She motioned her hand between us, and I felt my face get extremely hot when I realized what she meant by 'made up'. He set the brown bag down on the countertop and turned toward me.

Ignoring her comment, he said, "How are you feeling?" I

shrugged, trying to hide my flushed cheeks from him.

"Never better," I offered. He scoffed and went into the kitchen, emptying the bag out onto the counter.

"I went to get some stuff to make you something to eat to help with the hangover. My cooking is nowhere near as good as Jezebel's, but it'll do for now." No one said another word for what felt like an eternity until Emery chimed in.

"I've got an assignment tonight. They said they need a seer, and I could use some extra cash." He stopped what he was doing, a frown forming on his face.

"I can give you extra cash, Emery. I don't want you working for them." He sounded like a concerned older brother. She pressed her lips, her arms crossed over her chest defensively.

"Not everyone is good enough to just quit like you, you know." I knit my eyebrows together and she made a face. "He didn't tell you anything?" I shook my head. "Jeez, do you guys communicate at all?" I laughed, a nervous habit I had during serious moments.

"You were never even fully initiated," he corrected. "Just because you were asked a handful of times to help with something, doesn't mean you were a member. It's not the honor that you think it is."

She snapped, "You're so focused on everyone else, and you can't even get your own shit in order." She turned toward me; fury burrowed in her young features. "He fucking hates the Spiral but sought them out when he was trying to look for you. He 'retired' because he lost his shit until he found you in the diner and suddenly remembered that he had fucking feelings again." I watched his features twist into a sadness I had never seen in him.

"That's enough." His voice was harsh. She sighed dramatically.

"No, what's enough is the tension in this room. You spend

so much time trying to control and protect those around you instead of admitting to her how you feel because then it's out of your control. Just fucking apologize and get over it so that I can do my own thing without you breathing down my back." She walked over and snatched her keys off of the coffee table and stomped her way toward the door. "And you need to realize that your biggest hater, Arabella, is yourself. Get your shit together." As the front door slammed behind her, I could feel the silence in the room.

"I think she may have been upset with us," I joked but my voice sounded nervous. "Though I think she is pretty valid in her assessment." I could feel him watching me, but I kept my gaze down at my hands as I tried to think of what to say. "I don't really know how to do this, Keiran." He stayed quiet so I continued, my words coming out in a rush. "I've spent my whole life trying to prove that I wasn't worthless. I wasn't some weak little girl surviving purely off of a family name. I trained just as hard as you and Avery. Even with Damian." I paused for a moment but then kept going. "I never used the Blackwood or Stark name to better myself and yet I was still always made to feel like I had. And I was always reminded that nothing I did would ever be enough. So eventually, I just started to believe it and I hated that about myself."

"Arabella-" I held up my hand to stop him.

"I just need to get it out before I convince myself to keep it all in again." This time I met his gaze, and I could see all of the emotion he himself had hidden away. The anger, the sadness, the loneliness. "That night when we got into a fight, and you told me that I would never be good enough to be the wife of a Stark-" I felt the tears welling up and for once I didn't choke them back. Instead, I allowed myself to feel them. "I felt so fucking defeated."

CHAPTER TWENTY- ONE

Keiran

"I wanted to leave then because why should I continue to stay somewhere that I clearly wasn't wanted?" I was trying desperately to hold it together as the tears streamed down her face. I had never seen Arabella cry. I had seen the sadness in her face at times, the anger that she tried to contain. When I first met her, when I was 8 and she was 6, I stood there sulking and reserved as my mother introduced us and her father berated her for not throwing a punch correctly. She kept her face stoic, unreadable to seem as though she was unbothered by him displaying his shame for her. And I remember thinking that I admired her ability to hide it so well. How I wished that I could react the same every time my father put his hands on me.

But as we got older, I realized that it was just the wall she had put up to hide it so that they couldn't hurt her. I realized that she and I were a lot alike, and I wanted to protect her. Not just because I was told to but because I wanted to make sure that she didn't have to feel unworthy any longer. But then I did the same thing to her that they had done and only then did she actually cry.

"So, after I left you, I started to try and think of a plan on how to get out," she continued, trying to choke back a sob. "But every time I thought about it. Every time I thought about you and how your words were just a little too kind and your gaze would linger just a little too long. And I thought that maybe you were just trying to push me away like I was doing to you." She wiped her face, her tears slowing as she caught her breath. "But then I found you and Avery at the house and… a part of me was glad that it happened so that I wouldn't have to be conflicted." Her crying had stopped, and she huffed out a breath as if she was annoyed by her emotions at all. "But I was still angry because despite leaving and trying to act like you never existed-" Her voice dropped down to a whisper. "I'm still in love with you. And I was so caught up in my own anger that I never stopped to realize that you were hurting too." I could tell that she was trying to brush over the first part of what she said, like she didn't just tell me the one thing I've wanted to hear for the last 20 years. She had stopped speaking but for a moment all I could do was stare at her.

"I-" I was trying to form a coherent sentence. "Are you- are you trying to apologize for being angry at me?" As I said it, my phone started ringing loudly, filling the momentary silence between us but I quickly silenced it and kept my eyes on her.

"N-no. I just- I'm trying to admit that I was also wrong in how I handled things." The phone started ringing again. "It could be important. Maybe you should just answer it."

"I don't give a fuck about the phone, Arabella!" She flinched at my raised voice and tried to make herself smaller again, as if she was trying not to take up too much space. I wasn't angry at her, but I was angry. Angry at her family for making her a pariah, angry at Damian for making her flinch anytime someone touches her or gets too close. But most importantly, angry at myself for making her believe that her only option was to disappear. "I am the one who should apologize for making you fall in love with me and then betraying you; not once, but twice." The phone sounded again, and it took all my restraint not to chuck it across the room. Annoyed, I picked it up quickly. I kept my eyes on her as she kept looking at her hands, nervously fidgeting with them. "What the fuck do you want?"

Avery stammered, "I, uh. Malachi is back and he knows Arabella has returned. He's requesting an audience."

"Fucking fantastic," I sighed, pinching the bridge of my nose. "When?"

"Tomorrow evening. He said he wants a home cooked meal and some rest before dealing with the bullshit." I knew she spoke those words verbatim.

"Fine." I hung up and dropped the phone down on the counter rather harshly.

"Duty calls?" Her tone was lighthearted. I shook my head.

"Your father is back. And he wants to have a meeting." Her eyes shot up in a panicked expression. This was not going to go well, and she was fully aware of that. I knew this was why she wanted to avoid her family when she came back. What her father lacked in physical abuse, he sure made up for in mental and emotional abuse and you don't get to just disappear when you're a member of one of the First Families without some repercussions.

She said, "If I leave now, I could probably make it a few cities away before he could catch up." I shot her a begrudging look and she flinched. "I was just joking." She looked down at her hands again. I walked around the island counter and stepped in front of her, moving my hands to cup her face and force her to look up at me. My voice was low.

"I will spend the rest of my life trying to convince you that you are worthy of being loved, Arabella." I watched her fight back her tears. I wanted so badly to kiss her to stop her lower lip from quivering. "And I will not allow you to apologize for the way MY actions made you feel. I will fix this." I leaned down to kiss her forehead, and she closed her eyes as she put her hands on my chest. The moment was so intimate, and I wished that we could have been frozen in time like that. But we had to have this conversation. "In order to do that, however, we have to talk about that night." I could feel her demeanor change as she stepped away from me, the loss of contact feeling cold and uncomfortable. She crossed her arms over her chest and sat back on the arm of the sofa before taking a deep breath.

"It was a shitty night," she admitted with a sigh. I nodded and headed back into the kitchen, needing some distance between us. I started cutting up the vegetables I had gotten from the store to make her something to eat as I continued.

"One of the seer's had a vision about the Condemned." She sucked in a breath.

"Like from the stories?" I nodded again.

"They said that they were going to be reborn and that we needed to make sure that they couldn't find what they were looking for."

"The amulet?" I could see the pieces turning in her mind, like things were starting to make a whole lot more sense.

"Sort of." She knit her eyebrows together. I sighed as I set the knife back down and walked back out to the living room. She watched me curiously as I ran my finger along the bottom of the painting again, before typing in the code. 101797. Her birthday. When the safe popped open and I bent down to retrieve what I was looking for, my fingers hovered above it for just a moment as I thought of all of the things that had happened because of such a small brittle piece of worthless jewelry. Adorned with ancient runes, the thin metal chain was beginning to eat away at itself and the leather that bound it to the dark red gem at its head was flaking away as I held it. Her eyes shot up in realization before those green eyes turned deadly.

"You had it the whole time?" I walked over and placed it on the glass table. She hovered her fingers above it, not sure if it would fall apart at her touch. "Why were you pretending to help me then?" I sighed as I walked back into the kitchen to finish making dinner.

"I was trying to keep you safe. But in all honesty, I think I just wanted a reason to be near you, to make sure you didn't disappear again." Her gaze moved to me again, that guilt hiding in the back of those gorgeous eyes. "Before you get your hopes up, however, you should know that that amulet is completely useless." I went back to what I was doing, chopping up some onion and garlic before throwing them into a stainless-steel pan.

"Keiran, I don't care about eating. I want to know what you are talking about." I chuckled.

"I'll explain everything, Arabella. I promise. But you are going to eat." She rolled her eyes.

"You're so bossy sometimes." Her tone was exasperated. I scoffed but continued.

"That amulet belonged to the Condemned. It was created as a last-ditch effort to conceal some of his power so that he could come back after he was killed. But that amulet no longer has any power."

"Does that mean that he's already been brought back?" She had taken her place at the island between us, her head resting in her hands as she watched me. I smiled.

"You're very cute when you are focused."

"Anyway," she said, turning away to hide her blush. I smiled.

"Not exactly. Because the magick that was in it wasn't destroyed. It was transferred."

"To another object?" This time my fingers stilled on the

knife, my mind drawing me back to a memory.

CHAPTER TWENTY-TWO

I had been training since before the sun came up with my father and Damian that day. I had been exhausted, on the verge of collapse, by the time my mother intervened and told him that we needed to rest. That we could train again tomorrow. She was expressionless as she looked at Alexander, a hint of hatred in her eyes. She loathed him just as much as I did, regretted the day that her parents set up their arranged marriage to begin with. He had tried to push the issue, claiming that it was teaching us self-discipline, but she wasn't having it.

Elizabeth had been the complete opposite of her husband. Though she was just as strong, there was always a tenderness behind her eyes, a compassion that she held no matter how hard Alexander tried to beat it out of her. Especially for her children. It was such a harsh contrast between her gentle fingers running through my wet hair after I got out of the bath that night and the vice grip that Alexander favored during the day.

"When is father going to leave again?" I asked, my voice low in case he was close by. My mother sighed as she pulled a white t-shirt down over my 6-year-old head.

"Probably within the next few weeks," she admitted.

"I hate him." My words came out with such conviction as I crawled into bed, my small limbs and bones screaming from the excessive training.

"You shouldn't say that," Damian said from his bed across the room. He laid there with his eyes closed, his body facing the ceiling, and his arms folded underneath his light blond hair. The same color blond as our mother's. "He just wants us to be strong. You are just being a brat."

"Mother is strong, and she is nothing like him," I defended. "Why can't we train with you?" She sat on the corner of my bed, tugging the blanket up to my neck.

"Because your Aura isn't like mine," she said, a hint of sadness in her tone. "Your father can teach you how to use it better."

"You could teach me how to be a Seer too," I argued. "I'd rather use your magick than his." I sat up quickly, pulling on her arm. "You could take me with you tonight!" She shook her head, guiding me back under the blanket.

"You are too young to fight Necros, Keiran," she said.

"You should always be prepared to fight Necros," Damian said, his eyes now open as his attention was on us. "No matter how old you are." She kissed my forehead before standing and walking over to Damian and doing the same. He tried to act like he hated it, but I noticed the way he leaned into her when she kissed his head.

"And I'm sure your father has seen to preparing you in case the need arises. But I will not willingly take you out on a hunt. Especially one of this caliber. Maybe another time."

"Will tonight be dangerous?" The question came from Damian, something odd in his tone; the care that he once had still strong in him before Alexander beat it away.

"A hunt is always dangerous," she said, her voice serious. "Never forget that. Do you understand me?" She looked back and forth between us. We both nodded before she continued. "But tonight, we aren't just hunting Necros. We are looking for something."

"What is it?" My tone was almost excited but before she could answer, Alexander walked into the room, his emotionless eyes landing on his wife.

"Quit telling them stories," he said, his tone harsh. "They need to go to sleep so that we can train again in the morning. Besides, Jezebel is waiting for you downstairs. I hate that woman almost as much as I hate her husband so get her out of my house."

After a quick goodbye, my mother left, and we wouldn't see her again for a couple of days. When she did finally come back, you could tell that something was off. You could see the strain on her beautiful, gentle face, the sadness that encompassed her when she looked at us and for the longest time I never knew why. Two years after that night, we were finally introduced to the Blackwood family. And after I turned fifteen, when my mother was dying, that was when I learned what it was that she had been looking for that night. Or who she had been looking for.

"Keiran?" Arabella's voice brought me back to the present.

"S-sorry," I stammered. "What was I saying?"

"That the magick was transferred," she offered. I looked up at her again, a long moment of silence between us before I could admit to her everything that had been hidden from her since she was 4 years old. I took a deep, somber breath.

"It had been transferred to you, Arabella." She blinked in confusion, a slew of different emotions crossing her beautiful features.

"W-what do you- how?" I could tell she was desperately trying to find her words. "Why? I- what the fuck do you mean?" Her small hands gripped the granite countertop as if she were going to fall back if they hadn't.

"We aren't really sure why," I admitted, my face in a deep frown. "The night our mothers' went searching for the Amulet, they found it lying next to you. You were 4 years old then; just a tiny little thing that they found unconscious and surrounded by dead Mercenaries. It took them a few years to piece together that they had transferred it to you because there had been written pages that they had tried it on others, and it had failed." She stood up, pacing back and forth. Her brow was so furrowed together that I wasn't sure it would come undone.

"Okay. But- does that mean that Jezebel and the others were never actually my family?" Her eyes shot up, her jaw dropping as the realization hit her hard. I nodded. "I- I have so many questions, Keiran." As the protein in the pan started to sizzle, I placed a lid over it and walked over to her, my fingers moving to smooth out her creased brow. She stiffened but surprisingly, didn't pull away from my touch.

"I know, baby and I will answer every single one."

CHAPTER TWENTY-THREE

Arabella

Despite the instinct in me to shy away from physical touch, I leaned into Keiran, placing my hands on his chest as if to hold me up. My mind was spiraling, and I thought that at any moment, my legs were going to crumble from beneath me. His arms encircled my waist and suddenly I wasn't sure if his revelation was making me dizzy or his intoxicating scent. I leaned my head against his chest, unable to look into his eyes any longer without my mind going elsewhere. There were bigger problems right now than my need to get laid.

"No, the Blackwoods were never your real family." His voice was low in my ear. "The only reason you ended up in the life you did is because you had no one. No family, no ties to anyone that hadn't died placing this fucking curse on you. My mother didn't want you in our home because of Alexander and you looked just enough like Jezebel that you could pass as her daughter if anyone came asking. If anyone else had learned about you, about what you could do, the Spiral would have killed you." I felt like I couldn't breathe. I know it wasn't common to remember much of your toddler years. So, I didn't really ever question why I had no memories from before my 5th birthday but now it made so much more sense. The lies, the hatred that Avery held for me, the way they treated me like I wasn't one of them. Because I never was. I hadn't realized that I had started crying until Keiran lifted my chin and wiped away the tears from my cheek with his thumb.

"I was nothing more than a curse to them." I hated how small my voice sounded, how much their view of me affected me even now. How much I had craved their approval, and I was never going to get it no matter how hard I tried.

"You were a weapon," he said, his tone reluctant. "That's why Malachi had you train the way that he did. And when you left, they thought you were going to use it against them for the way they treated you. Which, you'd be well within your right to do so." He chuckled. I scoffed.

"I still could," I joked. "I've got a couple decades worth of pent-up frustration I could take out on them." He grinned, that seductive smirk back on his face.

"And how pent up is that frustration, Arabella?" I took a sharp inhale of breath, sucking my lip between my teeth. He cleared his throat, and I hadn't realized that my gaze had hyper focused on his lips. He moved his finger to pull my lip out from my teeth but those fucking blue eyes bore into mine like they were going to kill me.

"I- uh- I think the food is burning," I managed as the smell of burnt vegetables filled my nose.

"Fuck," he said, his voice husky and disappointed as he let go of me to run over and turn it off. His smile turned guilty. "I told you. I'm not good at this. I might have to order you something from door dash." I shrugged before wrapping my arms around myself, the sudden emptiness from the lack of his touch making me feel like I was going to float away.

"I'm not super hungry," I admitted. His face turned angry.

"You need to eat, Arabella," he said. "Something besides coffee and French fries. And it pisses me off that he fucking let you waste away. If he was so concerned about you 'doing his bidding' you would think he would have fucking made sure you were healthy enough to do so."

"That right there is why I couldn't compare you, you know," I said after a while, my voice low. His brow went up, unsure of where I was going with this. "Back at the club you asked me if I saw you in the same light as your father." I shook my head. "I don't. I never did because you were the only one that ever gave a shit. I just don't know how to accept it." He took a deep breath, and I could see him fighting the urge to walk over to me again. Although, it was probably a good thing that he didn't. If he looked at me like he did a few minutes ago, I was just going to tell him to fuck me against that window for the whole city to see.

"Don't worry, baby girl. I'm bossy, remember? I'll just have to make you accept it." I rolled my eyes.

It wasn't too much longer after that Liam showed up at the door with food containers in his hands. And even though I had said otherwise, when the smell of delicious Chinese takeout filled my nose, my mouth watered. Keiran didn't say much as we ate, just sat there and listened to me tell him about some of the things I had done in the last five years to pay back Alexander. Every so often, I'd notice the anger that he tried to hide at things that he had made me do and he admitted that some of the places that I had been, he went looking for me because someone had told him that I may have been the one he was looking for. But he had always shown up just a little too late. By the end of it, I felt exhausted.

"You should get some rest, love," he said as I laid my head against the back of the couch, a yawn escaping me. I rolled my eyes, but I was extremely tired and was going to take him up on the offer. Moving to lean against the armrest, I pulled my legs up underneath me and let my eyes lull shut. "What are you doing?"

"Going to sleep. I'm still imposing on you so I'm not going to take your bed again." He sighed.

"Arabella?" I opened my eyes, and he was watching me with a scowl on his face. "I will carry your ass back into that bedroom if I have to." I sat up, my eyes narrowing as I contemplated if I wanted to test that theory. I was feeling defiant.

"No." He lifted a brow.

"Stop fighting me on this. I'm not having you sleep on my couch." I shrugged.

"Guess I'm not sleeping then." His eyes turned deadly as he pushed away from the island. I shrank back into the couch, suddenly losing whatever balls I had a minute ago. He bent down, swooping me up bridal style, giving me zero chance to push away from him, and stalked back to his bedroom. He dropped me down on the bed, my ass landing with a soft thud before he disappeared into his closet. He came back out a moment later, a pair of sweats and a t-shirt in his hand before he closed the bathroom door behind him. He emerged a moment later, changed into his pajamas as he walked over to turn off the light. There was a slight cast of light through the window curtain from the moon, just enough to illuminate his amused face as he slid under the blanket next to me. "W-what are you doing?"

"Compromising. Now go to sleep."

CHAPTER TWENTY-FOUR

I didn't think that I could be any more aware of Keiran's presence than I was all night. I didn't want to fall asleep, afraid that I'd wake up wrapped around him not even meaning to. Well not consciously anyway. At some point, though, I did fall asleep and just as I thought I might have, the next morning I absently laid my arm across where he had been sleeping. When the space was empty, however, I shot upright, a sudden panic rising in my throat as I looked around the empty room. The bedroom door was open and just as I was about to get up, I heard his voice through it as he spoke to someone on the phone. I released a breath I hadn't known that I was holding and made a face. My breath smelled terrible!

I hurried into the bathroom to rummage through his medicine cabinet and drawers until I found some toothpaste. Using my finger as a makeshift toothbrush, I squeezed some of the paste onto my finger and ran it back and forth along my teeth and tongue as best as I could. I then used the mouthwash I found to swish around to kill any lingering scent. I cupped my hand around my mouth and nose, blowing into it to make sure it smelled like mint instead of a lingering hangover and the onion from last night's take out.

I was definitely going to have to get myself some necessities. What little I owned was left back at the Blackwood home and there was no way in hell that Malachi was going to let me back in to get it. I had a few hundred dollars to my name that I could use for a toothbrush and some clothes, but it wasn't enough to survive on for long. I was going to have to find a job but with the lack of Necro attacks recently, that wasn't going to be very easy to do. Not that it would even pay me enough to find a place to live. Could I even manage a regular life?

"What's wrong?" Keiran's voice pulled me out of my thoughts, and I hadn't realized that I had been staring at the ground absentmindedly. I shook my head.

"It's just- I don't really know what to do with myself now that I'm not working for him. Or doing something for someone." He grinned.

"You could just keep sitting there looking pretty. I'd be fine with that." I rolled my eyes.

"If you keep saying shit like that, I'm going to think you like me," I replied. He leaned against the door frame, his arms crossed over his broad chest and his sweats hanging low on his hips in a way that made my mouth dry up. His thick black hair looked like he had just run his fingers through it to push it back out of his handsome face, a few strands falling in front of his eyes as they roamed over me. He lifted an eyebrow.

"I don't like you, Arabella," he said, that morning gruffness still in his voice making it sound super sexy. "I'm in love with you. And you can't stand there and tell me that you don't feel the same."

"Well technically, I'm sitting so." I shrugged my shoulders, defiance on my face. I almost regretted it though when he pushed away from the door, closing the gap between us in the blink of an eye. I had zero time to react as he pushed my knees apart with his leg and tilted my chin up toward his face. Those blue eyes had darkened and were so full of lust I could feel it on my skin. I bit down on my lip and against my better judgement, moved my hands to rest on his lower stomach. He moved his hand to force my bottom lip from my teeth and ran his thumb along it, his eyes following the movement before moving back up to meet my gaze.

"We have to stop doing this," he said, his voice almost strained. I felt all the confidence I had a minute ago, deflate as I rolled my eyes. I pushed him away from me, getting up from the bed to walk out to the hallway. He followed behind me. "I'm trying to be a gentleman, Arabella." I rolled my eyes again with an audible sigh.

"I'm aware it's not all a ruse to get in my pants, Keiran. Maybe I don't want you to be a gentleman anymore. Maybe I just want you to fuck m-" Before I could finish what I was saying, Keiran spun me around and pinned me against the wall as his lips crashed against mine. I was taken aback, my mind almost refusing to believe this was happening until I felt him bite down on my lower lip. A soft, involuntary moan spilled from my mouth before my hands snaked their way into his hair, my lips parting to allow him better access. He tasted like mint, probably from the mouthwash that I found, as his tongue brushed against mine. He pushed his thigh between my legs, forcing them apart before his hands moved to the back of my thighs. In one swift movement, he lifted me off the ground, my ankles linking together as my legs wrapped around his waist. He never broke away from the kiss except for a small breath before finding his way back to my mouth like he was afraid I was going to disappear from his grasp. He kept one hand under me to hold me in place with the wall against my back and I felt all the breath leave my lungs when he moved the other to rub against my pussy over the outside of my sweats. I ground against his hand, craving his touch more than I needed a breath. He pulled away from me, pressing his forehead to mine as he grinned.

"Do you need some release, baby?" I couldn't speak, my breath uneasy as I felt the outline of his own arousal pushing against my belly button. I nodded my head. "You have to say it." I bit down on my lip again.

"Please touch me, Keiran." My voice was a low moan, but it was enough for him as he slid his hand into my waistband and his fingers hovered above where I desperately needed him to touch. He ran his finger along my slit, coating it in my arousal. I bucked against his hand, and he let out a low chuckle before he rubbed his middle finger against my clit in slow circular motions. I leaned my head back, my eyes lulling shut as his hand dipped lower, his thumb now rubbing circles as the other slipped inside of me, the two of them working in perfect unison. He kissed down my jawline and neck, placing a gentle kiss just below my ear.

"Do you know how often I think about what your moans would sound like?" His voice was rough, full of the promise of sex. "To hear you cry out my name?"

"Fuck," I breathed. I dropped my head, pressing my forehead against his shoulder to muffle another moan as it viciously tried to crawl its way out. His fingers slowed.

"Don't cover your face. Look at me, baby." I kept my head down, trying to keep myself in control. "Look at me now, Arabella." I shook my head, unable to speak. His fingers retreated, though he kept them hovering above my pussy, taunting me. "I won't ask a third time." A small whine escaped my lips, and I could feel how flushed my skin was as I slowly lifted my head to meet those deadly eyes. "Good girl." He grinned again as this time he slid two fingers inside of me. I cried out, my breathy moan filling the hallway as he picked up rhythm again. "Keep those pretty fucking eyes on me." I had moved my hands from his luscious hair down to his arms as if I were helping him hold me up. In actuality, I was about to crumble. I could feel my orgasm building, that sweet release just at the tip of this man's sinful fingers. He moved to bury his face in my neck, his forceful kisses lining my collar bone.

"Keiran." My moan was almost pleading.

"Fuck, baby say it again." I leaned my head back against the wall, struggling to keep my eyes on him. I didn't want him to stop. I needed it. Needed him. "Just lose control, baby girl." I wanted to, so fucking bad, and if this man had told me to come right then, I would have. But a knock at the door had me slamming my legs shut around Keiran. I snapped my head toward the front door as the sound of Emery's voice speaking to someone else carried through it. I felt the tip of my orgasm slip away, the embarrassment eating me alive as I pushed against him and he set me back down on my feet. I could see the disappointment on Keiran's face too. My gaze dropped down to the large erection pressing through his sweats and his eyes followed mine. He looked back up at me, that smug cocky grin on his face and I realized that I had unknowingly licked my lips.

I could hear Emery's key in the door, so I pushed him further away from me and started trying to fix my waistband and t-shirt. Keiran bolted behind the island as Emery and Sakura walked into the apartment, several large designer shopping bags in their hands. Emery had been speaking animatedly to Sakura until she stopped halfway through the living room, her perfectly shaped brows knitting together.

"Is everything okay? The energy seems a little thick in here." I almost choked on my own saliva as I stammered out a response.

"Yeah. We just- uh- were having a heated discussion about what we wanted for breakfast. I told him to just choose but he won't." Keiran's laugh was sinister as I looked at him. I nearly toppled over my knees when I saw him slide the two fingers that he just had buried inside of me, into his mouth, licking them clean.

"I'm very much aware of what I want to eat right now,"

he said, his eyes never leaving mine. My mouth fell open making him chuckle again.

"Well, we ordered food already so you're going to have to pick from that. It should be here soon, and we can eat while you pick out what you want to wear to tonight's meeting." Her response was so innocent, so unaware of what he really meant. As the two of them moved to set all the bags down on the couch, Keiran maneuvered his way back around the island.

"Save some for me," he said. "I need to shower."

"Wait," I whispered, making sure that the two of them were paying us no mind. He paused at my side, and still feeling some of the adrenaline from earlier, I stood on my tiptoes to kiss him quickly. "Hope you think of how wet I am while you're in there." My voice was incredibly low so that only he would hear me. A small, devious giggle escaped my lips as Keiran's eyes darkened. He gripped my arm, and I watched him physically fighting the urge to throw me over his shoulder and take me with him. Not that I'd mind... Emery's arm pushing against Keiran's back broke the silent standoff between us.

"Go away. Let us have some girl time." Unable to hide his erection any longer, he walked down the hall and into his bedroom, nearly slamming the door behind him in a hurry. She knit her eyebrows together as she looped her arm in mine, dragging me back toward the couch.

"What's his problem? Are you guys still fighting?" I shook my head, trying to keep my cheeks from giving me away.

"No, we actually talked," I admitted, trying to change the subject. "He's just brooding sometimes." She sighed dramatically.

"Thank the gods you noticed it too. I was beginning to think it was just me! Anyway, I don't think you guys were officially introduced yet so Sakura, this is Arabella. Arabella, this is Sakura." She offered a genuine smile, showing off her smiley piercing behind her perfect pale pink lips as she greeted me.

"Nice to officially meet you," she said, her voice kind. Sakura was genuinely one of the most beautiful people I had ever seen. Donning a white t-shirt cut to a crop and boyfriend jeans, her willowy arms held gracefully at her waist. Her deep brown curved eyes were accented by the black eyeliner she wore, and her flawless glass skin had just a touch of gold. Apart from the faded translucent scar that ran across her right cheek. I wondered if that was from Alexander and suddenly, I felt a huge rush of guilt from bringing that man back to the people that he had tortured.

"Nice to meet you, too," I said, returning a warm smile. "I really appreciate how much the both of you have been so nice to me despite me acting like a total bitch." Emery waved her hand and made a face as if to say all was forgiven.

"Water under the bridge. Just think of yourself as another member of the rat pack," Emery said and the three of us giggled. I had never really mastered the art of making friends in my life. I had Keiran and that was essentially it. Avery hated me so I never really knew what it was like to have a sisterly bond but there, at the back of my mind, I had a thought that maybe this was something like it. And suddenly, I found myself fighting back tears again.

"Now back to the task at hand. I know that you only like to wear black so everything we bought is right up your alley." She plopped down on the edge of the couch, pulling me down with her. "Keiran called this morning and told me that you didn't really have any clothing apart from what you had with you when you got here. He told me to get casual clothing as well as something formal in case the need arises. So, I think this one would be perfect for tonight since all council meetings are supposed to be formal." As she said it, she reached into a matte red shopping bag to pull out a beautiful strapless black tulle dress. The bodice looked like it would hug my breasts perfectly and the longer length would look great with some stilettos. But the fact that Keiran had already thought about me having to start over before I even did, despite how hard I tried to push him away, that fucking man was still there to fix it. And I loved him for it. "It's got thigh high slits on both sides to show off your legs. It would look fantastic with an updo and a dark red lip. You'll have every man panting at the sight of you."

I only wanted one man panting at the sight of me right now and I remembered the way he looked at me like he was going to take me right there in front of both Emery and Sakura, consequences be damned. He looked at me like he was damned to the underworld and only a taste of me would be his salvation. It didn't help that we never got to finish anything, so the need was still very much there, pooling between my legs and I wondered if he was still hot and bothered. Fuck, maybe I needed a shower...

CHAPTER
TWENTY-FIVE

Keiran

The cold water was doing fuck all to get rid of my hard on. No matter how hard I tried, all I could hear was her soft, desperate moans. All I could see was those emerald green eyes filled with a lust that matched my own. I wondered how good those eyes would look as she looked up at me with my cock in her mouth.

"Fuck," I said, sliding my dick into my hand. I should have had Arabella's silky hair wrapped around my hand as I fucked her from behind, telling her what a good girl she was for taking all of me. I should have had her on all fours as I ate her tight little pussy like it was my last fucking meal. And her little comment about thinking about how wet she is while I'm in here. Fucking wicked woman. I stroked my cock, a slow steady build up as I did as she said; thought about how wet she was when my fingers were inside of her. And how fucking delicious her arousal tasted. I needed to worship the ground she walked on, but I wanted to fuck her until she couldn't walk.

My breathing quickened. My hand slammed on the tiled shower wall as I stifled my own moans. My strokes were faster now, thinking of how I was going to make this woman mine in every way possible. And I'd start by finally making her my wife.

The idea hit me as my orgasm reached its head, my cock exploding into my hand and all across the tile. I hadn't realized how pent up I had been myself. It had been a while since I had gotten laid before I ran into Arabella in the diner. And the growing sexual tension between us had given me an intense case of fucking blue balls.

Then again, there was always a sexual tension between us. I just never took it there, despite wanting to and despite knowing the way she looked at me. Because it wasn't just about getting my dick wet with her. I wanted her in every sense of the word but, like her, I never thought that I was good enough. Until she told me that she was in love with me, and I knew at that moment that I was never going to be strong enough to let her go even if she had wanted me to. I was too selfish, and I didn't care as long as I had her.

I rinsed my arousal off myself as well as the tile before taking an actual hot shower. I tried to avoid thinking about her because every time I did, I'd feel him try to spring forward again. I had shit to do and couldn't spend all morning rubbing one out in the shower. I finished up quickly and got dressed, donning an all-black suit with a matching silk tie to match whatever dress Arabella was going to wear. She had always favored wearing black. It was such a stark contrast between it and her beautiful porcelain skin, but it suited her. Red was also a breathtaking color on her especially when she wore it on those full, tempting lips. The thought had my pants tightening and I had to resituate them before walking back out to the living room.

It was quite the scene. Emery was speaking around the food in her mouth as she vehemently argued with Sakura about which character in the JJK anime was more attractive, Gojo or

Geto. Emery chose Gojo while Sakura defended that Geto had that shadow daddy vibe. Whatever the fuck that meant. But Arabella sat quietly, and despite looking slightly confused on who was who, she had a genuine, gorgeous smile on her face as she watched them. My little band of strays as she called them. Our little band of strays.

"Having fun?" I asked, walking up behind Arabella on the couch. She leaned her head back, looking up at me at a backwards angle.

"We are educating Arabella on which sorcerer is the best," Emery said, spooning another bite of potatoes into her mouth.

"Any takeaways?" I asked, looking down at her. She shrugged.

"Probably Geto since I seem to prefer the black haired, pensive type." Her little giggle was so fucking cute as she said it that I couldn't help it as I bent down and kissed her. As I pulled back slightly, her eyes were up in shock and her cheeks were flushed. I laughed as she moved her head back to a forward position and both Sakura and Emery were looking at us in amusement.

"It seems you figured your shit out," Emery taunted with a laugh, using the words she had used the day before. "It's about fucking time."

"Well not completely," I admitted. "I've got something I need to take care of." Arabella looked back up at me.

"You're leaving?" Her eyes slid shut as I bent down and kissed her forehead.

"Just for a little bit. And then I'll be back for you."

I kissed her again before grabbing my keys from the glass bowl on the table by the door and heading out. I drove illegal speeds to get across town. I hated going to the Boneyard, but I needed to see the Elders and ask them to grant a union between Arabella and I. Preferably within the next couple of hours. And not just because I wanted to marry her right away. But because a union would make whatever plan Malachi Blackwood was concocting for this council meeting, null and void. Not only would she no longer be under any control he thought he had, but she'd also be the wife of the Proctor which meant she was virtually untouchable. Except by me because I was going to touch every fucking inch of her, so she'd make those sexy little sounds again.

I stopped just on the edge of town, a small spiraling dirt path that passed through the rugged green forestry. What looked like an untouched hiking route through the woods was really an entrance, hidden by powerful magick that separated the Elders from the rest of the world. I got out of the car, pulling my phone out of my pocket to send a text to Arabella.

Me: You looked so pretty when you were about to come. You're going to look breathtaking when your legs are on my shoulders and I'm buried inside of you.

I tucked the phone back into my suit pocket before walking toward the entrance. It was the end of September, the last warmth of the summer season clinging on with frail fingers. But as I stood in front of the Boneyard, the magick was bitingly cold, eating up the exposed skin of my hands and face with frozen teeth. I shivered involuntarily before reaching my palms toward the invisible entry way. It was only a matter of seconds before I felt it; a long wet slippery tongue gliding across both palms, drawing blood in its wake. It stung, like pouring salt into an open wound. But the blood was what was needed to open the pathway. Like throwing a stone into calm waters, the barrier rippled, allowing me to step through and run right into someone's back covered in a silk white robe. I heard Elysium's grunt as he slowly turned around.

"You must give me time to get out of the way, Keiran," he said, his sonorous voice muffled as he licked my blood from the corner of his grotesque mouth. He moved his hands in front of him, his long, marred fingers clasping together slowly. He looked at me, his inhuman height forcing him to look down despite me being 6'3, giving me a full view of the blue illuminated spiral carved into his forehead.

"I need you to grant me a union." Elysium's thick blackened eyebrow raised in amusement.

"Keiran Stark wants a wife?" He made an odd sound, one that I could only attune to being a laugh. "And who would that be?"

"Arabella Blackwood." He inhaled sharply, making a whistling sound with his teeth.

"I hear she is an impulsive, feisty little thing. Now that the prodigal daughter has returned, she'd make quite an asset to the Spiral."

"She will not be joining the Spiral." My tone was harsh, warning him not to push it. He laughed again.

"Relax, Keiran," he offered. "I was simply thinking out loud."

"Think quieter," I retorted. He grinned, large, blackened teeth staring back at me. He held up his hands in surrender.

"I will grant you the union."

"I need it done today." Elysium turned away from me, the sound of his large feet shuffling across the dirt ground.

"Then bring her here and I will see to it."

With that I turned and walked back through the barrier, its cold temperature enveloping me until I was completely through it. It dissipated again, turning back into a scenic route as I walked back to my car. I hopped in the driver seat, pulling my phone back out of my pocket to see a message from Arabella.

Her: I'd be even prettier on top so you know I'm the one in control.

CHAPTER TWENTY-SIX

Arabella

"You really do have great tits," Sakura said as I turned around a few times, trying to show them the full view of the dress. The bodice was snug, barely concealing the fact that I had no bra underneath.

I laughed, "If you keep complimenting me like that, I might have to choose you over Keiran." Emery shrieked dramatically.

"He'd literally kill you, Sakura," she said as they both giggled.

"Yeah, I'm not trying to die just yet," she added with a huge grin. As she said it, I heard my phone ping from the couch. I opened it to find a message from Keiran.

Him: You looked so pretty when you were about to come. You're going to look breathtaking when your legs are on my shoulders and I'm buried inside you.

I bit down hard on my lip, trying to conceal the squeal

that wanted to come out of me. I had been good this whole time, not thinking- too much- about this morning. Emery and Sakura were actually very good at keeping my mind occupied on the task at hand. But holy shit the thoughts running through my head right then. It scared me how much I wanted this man and suddenly the thought made me nervous as I typed out my reply.

Me: I'd be even prettier on top so you know I'm the one in control.

I set the phone back down on the couch and turned back to them.

"No, he wouldn't," I defended absently but they both gave me knowing looks.

"Deny it all you want but that man is smitten," Emery laughed as she handed me a plastic Sephora bag filled with brand new makeup. Was there anything this girl didn't think of? She managed to get clothes, shoes, makeup, even bras and panties and claimed it was just 'a few items to hold me off'. Then again, she did have the ability to see things, so she had an advantage I suppose. "And don't pretend like we can't see the hickey on your collarbone. You're just as guilty as he is." I did notice the hickey when I went and showered before changing into the dress and I mentally cursed Keiran out every which way possible for it because it was going to be hard to hide. I blushed and turned away from them. I left the two of them giggling on the couch to go do my makeup for tonight.

I did my usual pinup style with a sharp winged eyeliner, blush, and a deep red lip. I was concentrating really hard to cover up the hickey when I heard an appreciative groan from behind me. I looked up to see Keiran through the mirror, his arms crossed over his chest as he leaned against the door frame, his eyes roaming up and down my body, focusing on the two slits that ran dangerously high up my thighs. I flushed red, trying to hide the embarrassment on my face as I turned back to trying to hide the hickey.

"This is really hard to cover up," I said, trying to come off as annoyed.

"Then don't hide it," he said, his voice sounding husky and low. I met his gaze through the mirror and rolled my eyes.

"Yeah, that would make a great impression on Malachi and make him not want to kill me." He pushed away from the doorframe, his arm snaking around my waist, pulling me flush against his front. I took a sharp inhale of breath, taken off guard as his lips trailed along my shoulder. I leaned my head back against his chest, a soft moan escaping me involuntarily.

"Are you sure you're in control, Arabella?" he breathed, his warm breath against my skin making me shudder. He gently trailed his kisses from one shoulder to the other, each one slow and deliberate as if he was savoring them all.

"Keiran," I breathed, my eyes closing as I leaned further back against him. He let out a quiet snort, letting me know that he knew I wasn't in control of anything right now.

"You're always so restricted," he said between kisses. "With what you do." Another kiss. "With what you say." Another. "With how you act." Another. "And with who gets to see the real you. But this-" He moved his hand from around my waist to slide through one of the slits in the dress. His fingers grazed between my thighs, feeling my arousal through the thin fabric of my thong. "Your pleasure? That's my responsibility, baby. And you're going to lose control for me." A whimpering sound ripped out of me as he pulled away from me, leaving me still wanting from earlier. It was borderline edging at this point... A wicked grin spread across his face. "Soon baby. But right now, we gotta go." I knit my eyebrows together in confusion, trying to hide how weak my body was from need.

"The meeting isn't for another 2 hours. Where are we going?" His smirk was beaming now.

"I told you; you still owe me a wedding."

As he pulled me back through the living room and out the front door, calling out over his shoulder to the others that we'd see them later, I tried to argue with him. Tried coming up with every excuse on why I'd make a terrible bride. But as we drove across town, he was having none of it.

"I thought you were just joking," I admitted, my fingers twirling in my lap nervously as I watched him. But that smug grin never left his face.

"I've wanted to marry you since we were children, Arabella. It's not a joke."

"Yeah but-" I paused, moving to rest my elbows on my knees as I pinched the bridge of my nose. "Everything that has happened. I just- why?"

"There are a multitude of reasons but let's start with the logical ones since you seem to be able to grasp that better." His tone sounded annoyed that I refused to believe he really wanted this. "If we were to get married, it makes it so that Malachi cannot do anything to you." My eyes shot up as I looked at him again. "You'd no longer be a Blackwood which means he would have no say over anything to do with what happened. And on top of that, you'd be the wife of the Proctor which means you will out rank even him." I opened my mouth to speak but closed it again, so he continued. "Not to mention, the Spiral approves of the union because they think I've got their best interests in mind. Which means they are less likely to come asking questions that we don't exactly have answers to."

"Does that mean that you aren't leaving the Spiral yet?" There was a sadness in my voice. The emotion that crossed his face was gone just as quickly.

"If I stay, then I will know whatever move they make. The Spiral's whole objective has always been to resurrect the Condemned so they can kill him once and for all and if they found out that you held the power to do so, they'd kill you." I took a slow, drawn-out breath. He was right; they were some pretty solid fucking reasons. But I hated that once again, this man was forced into a position because of me... "But on the emotional side of things," he said, his tone lighter as he tried to change the subject. "I've been madly fucking in love with you, Arabella, since you looked me in the face and told me that I hit like a bitch."

CHAPTER TWENTY-SEVEN

It was after Elizabeth's funeral. Malachi was screaming at me, his hot breath splaying across my face with pure disgust because my Aura had run out before I could even attack Keiran during our sparring match. My father said I was too distracted and that 'my inability to retain useful fucking information was going to get me killed'. I was pissed off. Not only because of Malachi's words but because Keiran was looking at me with that stupid smug face of his. That was the only emotion he would fucking show since his mother had died and right then, I had the need to wipe it off his face.

I lunged for him, but he managed to dodge it, dipping to the side and coming back with an uppercut that hit me square in the jaw. Blood filled my mouth and Keiran's laugh cut through my momentary daze. Malachi had made a comment about proving his point, but I ignored it as I spit blood at Keiran's feet.

"How am I supposed to learn real combat when you hit like a bitch, Stark," I said, meeting his gaze with defiance and suddenly, that was the first smile I had seen on his face in weeks.

Keiran grabbed my hand, pulling me back to the present and I realized we were parked in front of what looked like an abandoned hiking trail, remnants of a used path that was starting to be reclaimed by the forest around it. I looked back at him.

"Are you taking me out here to murder me?" His laugh was boisterous as he let go of my hand to get out of the car. He met me at the passenger side as he opened the door for me and held his hand out toward mine. I swatted his hand away as I got out of the car. The energy felt off, however, as I stepped a few feet in front of him and he closed the door behind me. It was at least in the mid-70s outside, low enough that you could feel the changing season in the air while still tasting the last remnants of the summer breeze. But as we stood at the front of the old path, my arms and legs were riddled with goose bumps, a bitingly cold breeze brushing over them forcing me to shiver. "Where are we?"

"The Boneyard," he said. "Only an Elder can perform a union. But you have to be willing, Arabella." I turned back to look at him and for the first time since the moment I met Keiran Stark, there was an uncertainty in his face as he looked down at the little black box he held in his hand. An uncertainty because he wasn't sure that I was willing to do this. Was I?

Was I willing to be thrown back into the world that I had run away from? I had unconsciously been asking myself this question since I came back, since I saw Keiran in the diner, and I realized that I never let go of this man the way that I thought I did. I took a deep, shaky breath, fighting back tears when I saw the longing in Keiran's eyes.

"Yes." My voice was so low I wasn't sure he heard me. But his eyes went up, the hopefulness thrashing around his face like a violent storm.

"Yes what, Arabella?" He took a step toward me, the box now sitting open as the skylight hit the diamond ring just right, a beautiful tangerine reflection bouncing off of it. My breath caught in my throat again as I recognized that ring. His mother's ring. She had joked before she died that it was going to be a grueling process but that the ring was going to be mine one day. Only now as I looked back up to meet his eyes again, I realized that it was never intended to be a joke.

"Yes, I'll be your wife." He closed the distance between us in one step, grabbing me and pulling me against him like we were tethered to each other. He kissed me, the taste of his desperation soaking his lips. My arms slid around his neck, my sudden need to get closer to him driving my fingers through his hair with malicious force, as I was unable to fight back the tear that slid down my cheek.

"So sorry to interrupt." A resonant voice came from behind us, pulling Keiran away from me. I turned around, met only by the empty trail and confusion. "We do have a deadline do we not?" I turned back toward Keiran, his face annoyed as he slipped his arm around my waist, pulling us forward. He stopped just in front of the trail, letting go of me long enough to hold his palms out in front of him.

"Hold your hands out like this," he said to me. Hesitantly, I did as he said but nearly shrieked when I felt something wet and cold glide across my palms, burning them in its wake. I pulled them back, blood pooling as I looked down at them.

"What the fuck was that?" Before he could answer my question, it was like the area in front of us tore through the fabric of time. What was once a beautiful place overrun with nature rippled and transformed into a cold barren flat land littered with red dirt and scattered bones. It was quiet, eerily so as the only sound was that of the wind that whistled by, almost resembling distant screams, and the air was thick and stagnant. But there, not but maybe 10 feet in front of us stood 5 huge, hooded figures. They held their arms out at their sides, the marred skin stretching over their long thick splayed-out fingers and their heads held down almost as if in a prayer.

"Elysium." As Keiran called his name, the hooded figure directly in the middle stepped forward. I bit back a scream as his head snapped upward, his large inky black eyes meeting mine with authority. He moved his large head back and forth, long silver white hair falling down in strands around his disfigured face and the vibrant blue spiral carved into his forehead was almost glowing.

"From your little display, I'm assuming both of you are willing to go forward with this union?" As he spoke, I realized his was the voice that we had heard before the entrance to the Boneyard had opened. Keiran nodded and Elysium came closer, almost completely closing the distance between us with one stride of his long legs. Before I knew what was happening, his huge hand was gripping my arm, pulling me to stand directly in front of him as he inhaled the air around me. Instinctively, I pulled back, barely managing to pull my arm out of his grip. If he really wanted to, he could have crushed me with one go. "I could taste the power in your blood, Arabella. Even the air around you tastes sweet with it." Keiran's face faltered for a moment, the thought of them finding out the truth hanging between us. "I wonder what we could accomplish if you were to become a member of the spiral."

"I already told you, that's not fucking happening," Keiran snapped, not nearly as visibly terrified of this thing as I was. Elysium chuckled, I think, as it sounded more like a death rattle before he took a step back.

"Arabella is perfectly capable of making her own decisions, is she not? Although, I expected more words from the girl that killed Damian Stark." I crossed my arms over my chest defensively.

"I'm trying to think of a more respectful way to tell you to go fuck yourself," I said. I don't know what I was expecting him to do but he started laughing again, this time almost manically as he threw his hands together, their large form making a deep, ringing clap sound.

"Oh, I like her! The two of you are going to be a wonderful

power couple." In a swift movement, he grabbed Keiran by the arm. He dragged his long, pointed thumbnail down his forearm, pulling with it a thick black line of Keiran's Aura before dropping the arm back down by his side. I tried not to flinch as he did the same to me, drawing a deep red line of my own Aura before letting me go.

Both Keiran and I watched in silence as both colors swirled around in Elysium's upturned palm. He leaned his head back slightly, the pale skin around his eyes blinking uncontrollably as the magick sliced into his palm, drawing blackened blood that seemed to settle at the tips of his fingers. Suddenly, he went limp, his body hunching forward with closed eyes, and it grew eerily quiet again.

I was half tempted to reach out and touch him when he shot upright, grabbing both Keiran and I's hands. He forced our palms upright before digging his nail into the flesh, our own blood spilling out onto our skin once again and I realized that this was almost identical to being Bound. Was that what Keiran had meant about having to be willing? Because if I wasn't then it would have been just as painful as when Alexander Bound me to him. Only, Alexander hadn't taken any of my Aura in return.

A warm, electric feeling shot through my veins, pulling me back from unwanted thoughts. The last remnants of our combined energies spilled through the open wound in my palm before Elysium stepped back, his face unreadable and otherworldly once more. Keiran reached for my hand, his healing spilling over it the moment his skin touched mine, but he kept his eyes on the Elder in front of us.

"Is it done?" he asked, his tone stoic. The Elder attempted what I think was a smile, large, blackened teeth hanging over thin lips.

"The union is complete."

CHAPTER TWENTY-EIGHT

Keiran

"I was expecting a longer process if I'm being honest," Arabella said as I slid into the driver's seat after closing the door for her. I shrugged as I threw the car in reverse and sped off back toward town.

"There's usually more of a celebration but I didn't think you'd want any of that."

"You were right in that assessment," she said, though the little smile on her face as she reached for my hand said as much. The thought of being on display in front of people that I really didn't care for so that they could judge how much money was spent and how long they'd think the union would last. I shuddered at the thought myself. I smiled as I brought her hand up to my lips, kissing her soft fingers.

"And here I thought that it was an unspoken rule that wives always disagreed with their husbands," I joked, keeping her hand in mine as I set it in my lap.

"Oh, don't worry. I'm still going to have an attitude 99% of the time."

"Fuck, I hope so. Though, I'll never be able to get anything done." She looked at me with a puzzled look. "You have spent your entire existence creating this hardened, fortified persona. You have a need to be defiant and combative because you were forced to be and that need mirrors my innate desire for you to let go, Arabella. I want you to enjoy it when I'm in control and fuck you into submission. If you've always got an attitude, it's going to make me a very busy man." My grin turned devious as she sucked in a breath, pulling that fucking bottom lip into her teeth. I reached up and pulled it from their grasp, the deep red lipstick she wore hiding the assault on her flesh, and battled my inner desire to take her back home instead of to this fucking meeting. As if I needed another reason to hate Malachi.

"I- uh." She blushed as she stammered over her words before letting out an exasperated sigh. "Fuck, I wish we could bypass this meeting," she said finally, mirroring my exact thoughts. Me too, baby. Me too.

She didn't really say anything else as we drove to our destination. Though, every so often I could feel her watching me. I had looked back a few times and she'd look away shyly and I couldn't help the shit eating grin that would stake its claim across my face. She was so fucking beautiful, and she was my fucking wife. I could almost hear Elizabeth's voice telling me it was about fucking time.

As we pulled onto the narrow driveway that led up to the old sacred building at the top of the hill, however, I felt her energy shift. Her hand stiffened in mine as her eyes glued to the old building in front of us, the oil lanterns illuminating the heavy large red door below them and the green moss that ate its way up the ancient stone was dry and uninviting. We were the first to arrive.

"I'm afraid of what he might try and do," she said, her

voice small. I leaned toward her, pulling her face toward mine as I gently gripped her chin. This time she didn't flinch or pull away.

"If he is stupid enough to try something, I'll be right there with you." She gave me a small smile before she audibly sighed again. She sat patiently as I went and opened the door for her, this time taking my hand instead of swatting it away like she did at the Boneyard. She followed behind me as we walked up the small stone steps to the building. Using my free hand, a thick inky black tendril spilled from my palm and wriggled its way toward the middle of the door. With a heavy force, it crashed directly into the wood before splintering out across the whole door, like the roots of a tree seeking a water source until they sprang back toward the middle.

"That's new," she said, her voice curious as I pulled the tendril back into my palm.

"I added it as an extra security measure. The door will only respond to my Aura."

"Did something happen?"

"We keep sensitive information here and I didn't think it a great idea to leave it so accessible to those that may have ill intent. The Spiral doesn't care about anything that doesn't involve them or their objectives so if anyone were to ever get in here and steal something then there would be no repercussions apart from what I am capable of."

"Gotcha." As she said it, the door swung open, the cool stagnant air from the dusty old stones spilling out from the inside. Arabella shivered, pulling herself further into my side. I let go of her hand to put my arm around her waist.

'Shall we?"

CHAPTER TWENTY-NINE

Arabella

I always hated coming here. Though things may have been different, it didn't help me think of anything other than the shitty memories this place held. I hadn't been here often, only ever having stepped foot in here when Malachi was trying to make a lesson out of me for the other kids. It was always because I had done something wrong, and my father wanted to display my failures in front of them, so they knew what a Mercenary wasn't supposed to be like.

My body instinctively filled with dread as we walked down the red velvet covered hallways, dimly lit by crystal shaped lights lining the bitter stone walls. It felt as stagnant as I remembered. Since it was all made of stone and there were no windows, scents lingered for far too long and the smell of burnt candles danced around us like a barrier. The hallways branched off into other rooms but the one we were in now was where all council meetings were held. In the center sat a huge rectangular wooden table, said burnt candles sitting in the middle and 4 large red wooden chairs on both sides with another one at each end, making 10 in total.

I could feel Keiran watching me as I walked along the table, running my fingers along the old wood before stopping at the head of it. He followed and took the seat that I was standing in front of before I turned to face him.

"I hate this place." I admitted. "I wonder if the view is any different from your seat of power, Mr. Proctor." His smirk was devious as he uncrossed his arms and leaned toward me, trailing his hand along the back of my thigh until he reached my ankle. He yanked it forward, placing my heeled foot down on the seat between his thighs as I leaned back against the table.

"The view is pretty fucking great from where I'm sitting," he said, his voice husky as his fingers trailed back up along my calf. I pulled back and moved to press my stiletto into his chest, trying to convey whatever self-control I thought I had. His head dipped as his fingers grasped my ankle again, his lips pressing gently against the skin there. His eyes rolled shut as he took a deep inhale through his nose. "Fuck, you smell good."

"I'm hanging on by a thread here, Keiran," I whispered, my voice shaky. He opened his eyes, his face mischievous as he met my gaze and let go of me, dropping my ankle back down to the floor.

"Take off your panties." I stared at him.

"Are you crazy?" I stammered over my words. "The meeting starts in like 30 minutes. What if someone shows up early?" The smile on his face never faltered as he replied.

"They usually don't but on the off chance they did, they'd get one hell of a show." I felt the heat in my cheeks.

"I- wh-" I motioned toward the space around us. "Isn't this a sacred place?"

"Then I'm going to desecrate it by sitting your ass on this table and burying my face between your thighs. Now take.

Them. Off." My mouth fell open, a mix of shock and arousal barely keeping me standing as he moved the chair closer to me. "There is now only 28 minutes left, Arabella." I took a deep, shaky breath as I slowly hooked my fingers into my thong, my brain going a thousand miles a minute. The fabric felt like a live wire brushing across my skin as I slid them down my thighs. His eyes followed the movement, his thumb brushing across his lower lip as they dropped, and I stepped out of them. His eyes met mine as he leaned down to snatch them off the ground before tucking them into the front pocket of his suit jacket. Running his hand along the back of my thigh again, he hooked it under my knee, pulling it up to his mouth with much less patience than he had earlier. I pressed further back against the table, the only thing keeping me from crumbling to the ground as he kissed along the exposed skin of my inner right thigh.

"Keiran." His name spilled from my tongue like it was the only word it knew.

"Hm?" he muttered, his warm breath dancing across my skin. I felt my leg buckle as I gripped the table. He chuckled, standing to his feet before lifting me up onto its surface. He pressed his hands down flat on either side of me, his face inches from mine as he met my gaze. "I'm going to fucking devour you, Arabella." His lips crushed mine with a force that took my breath away before they trailed down my neck and chest. My fingers tangled in his hair, a small desperate plea to never be separated from it again. As his lips trailed possessive kisses between both breasts, another groan of approval escaped his lips. "You really do have great fucking breasts." I giggled. "Is that amusing?" I shook my head.

"Sakura thought so too," I said, my voice a mix of humor and desperation. His kisses trailed down my stomach as he bunched the fabric of my dress up around my hips.

"Hmm should I be jealous?" I shrugged. "I like Sakura. Don't make me kill her."

"I mean, she is gorgeous. Could you blame me?" His laugh was seductive as his arms hooked around my thighs to pull me closer to him, his lips placing a soft kiss just above my pubic area. I felt him blow slow, deliberate breaths against my exposed skin, my arousal creating a cold sensation that made me shiver in anticipation. I could hear the amusement in his voice as he spoke.

"What did I tell you about that sarcasm, Arabella?" My back arched unprovoked, my need to be touched by this man making me feral.

"Please, Keiran," I pleaded, no longer holding on to any type of restraint. A low, greedy growl left him as his tongue dipped into my pussy and back up to brush against my clit. A desirous moan escaped me as my head fell back against the table.

"You're so wet for me, baby." My hips bucked in response before his arms tightened around my thighs, pinning my ass to the table. It felt like an eternity before he was on me again, sucking the sensitive bud back into his mouth. He swirled his tongue around it and sucked, and the sound that left my lungs was unholy. Keeping one arm still firmly holding me in place, his other moved between my thighs, his fingers heating my skin in their wake, before slipping one of them inside of me. "So fucking wet."

He withdrew his finger slowly, painfully so, before sliding back in again, this time curling it upward and moving it back and forth like he was telling someone to come to him. My fingers tightened in his hair like they were going to keep my soul from leaving my fucking body.

I could feel my orgasm building as my low moans were getting desperate. Trying to bite it back, I threw my arm over my face, burying it into the crook of my elbow as his tongue dipped lower again, moving in perfect sync with his hand. In one swift movement, though, he pulled out of me and sucked my clit between his teeth, nipping it in a move that skated the thin line between pleasure and pain. I nearly leapt off the table if it hadn't been for him holding me still. His husky voice was hot against my core.

"What did I say about covering your face?" My breath was uneven as I leaned forward on my elbows to meet his ravenous gaze. Fuck, this man was going to make me stupid with that look alone. Let alone his tongue. "That's my good girl." His attention moved back to his task at hand as he suctioned that fucking mouth back on my clit, this time without using his teeth, and I realized I definitely had a praise kink. I suppose it made sense. I'd spent my entire life seeking approval from places I'd never get it. And here he was, praising my very existence with that wicked mouth and I clung to those words like they were the very thing keeping me alive.

"Oh god," I moaned as Keiran's hand slid between my thighs again, pushing two fingers inside me to pull me from my train of thought. With each thrust, he slid them deeper, rubbing that sensitive spot slowly before he'd pull out again. I rolled my hips in rhythm, earning an enthusiastic growl from him.

"Mm, that's right, baby," he groaned. "Show me how much you need it." My body arched like it was fucking possessed by a demon itself as I felt the tension coiling deep inside me.

"Fuck, Keiran. I can't-" He tore a throaty moan from my lungs as his pace quickened, his mouth just as unrelenting as his fingers. He only let up enough to speak.

"Just let go, Arabella." And then I fell apart like my body was waiting for those four words. I threw my hand over my mouth, biting down hard into my palm as the orgasm ripped through me. His movements didn't stop as he rode it out with me, continuing until my body was no longer convulsing. My breathing was quick, sporadic like I had forgotten how to breathe at all as he stood up. He scooped his arms under my ass, pulling me to the edge of the table to wrap my legs around his waist. I met his hungry gaze, his mouth and chin soaking wet from eating me out, and nearly choked when he pulled my panties from his pocket and used them to clean his face.

"You missed a spot," I said, my tone playful as my eyes focused on the corner of his mouth. He used his thumb to swipe at the area and brought it up to his lips. "Wait." I grabbed his hand, keeping my eyes on his as I ran my tongue along the length of his thumb and sucked it into my mouth, swirling my tongue around it before slowly popping it back out. His pupils dilated, that same look he gave me back at the apartment when Emery showed up, darkening his face. "I got it."

CHAPTER THIRTY

Keiran

I was struggling with my self-control. That was the hottest fucking thing I'd ever seen. My cock had already been straining in my pants so bad it was bordering painful and now I was ready to piss off the whole council to take her home and fuck her pretty little brains out. It was almost enough to make me forget that she had still muffled her cries when she came on my face despite me warning her not to. Almost. She let go of my hand long enough for me to wrap it around her, pulling her as close as our bodies allow as I kept my face serious.

"Didn't I tell you to stop covering your face?" Her face, still flushed and beautiful from her orgasm, turned guilty.

"I-" I kissed her, stopping her apology before it could leave her lips. I hoped she could taste herself on my tongue too, so she knew how fucking delicious she was.

"You have this habit," I said, pulling away and pressing my forehead to hers. "Of trying to make yourself small. Of suppressing your own feelings or needs so you don't upset anyone. I'm going to break it." I bowed my head lower, placing a kiss on her neck before whispering in her ear. "And when you come, whether on my fingers, on my tongue, or on my fucking cock, you're going to tell me how good it feels." A squeal escaped her mouth, making me chuckle as I came back up to meet her gaze. "Do you understand me?" Her eyes went big, a breathtaking swirl of dark and light green that danced with desire. She nodded before her small fingers snaked into the lapels of my suit jacket, pulling me closer to her. I kissed her again, this time a lot more aggressive as my hands moved to her hips. My phone pinged on the table and without pulling away from her, I glanced down to see a message from Mr. Khumalo, telling me that he and his son had arrived. Not that I didn't already know that since I could feel their Aura the moment they got close enough. I groaned. "I really want to say fuck this meeting and take you home." She smiled against my lips.

"Then why don't you?" Her voice was low and sexy, driving my dick fucking wild.

I sighed, "It would be awfully unprofessional of me since the others are here." Her eyes went wild again, this time in embarrassment as she pushed me away from her.

"Why didn't you say something sooner? They could have walked in here!" She hopped down off the table, dropping her dress down around her delicious thighs as she tried to smooth it out before hitting me in the chest. There was a look of annoyance on her face, the kind that made me want to lay her back down on the table and taste that delectable little cunt of hers again until it was gone. Fuck, I had it bad. I held up my hands in mock surrender.

"I only just saw the message. Besides, only I can open the door. Remember?" I laughed at the expression on her face, and she narrowed her eyes at me.

"You could have said that earlier. Give me my panties back." She held her hand out and I smiled devilishly.

"No." As she stood there gaping at me, I released my Aura again, its thick black energy snaking its way down the hallway until it reached the door we had come in through.

"What do you mean no?" She snapped, her pissed off tone just too cute. I pulled her to me again, bowing my head so I could kiss her.

"I think I'll hold onto them." My tone was humorous as my aura sprung back to me. "Think of it as payback for not allowing me to hear you come." I stifled my amusement by the rage that crossed her face. She opened her mouth to speak but snapped it shut when Mr. Khumalo and his son joined us in the room.

"Keiran," Kijani said, his deep Swahili accent cutting through the tension. "It's good to see you again." My smile was huge as I slid my arm around her waist and pulled us both around the table to greet them. Kijani and his son, Akida, were a spitting image of one another. Both tall and broad shouldered, the calm demeanor that radiated off them filled the space between us.

"The honor is mine, Kijani." I extended my other hand, gripping his in a firm, friendly handshake. "And you as well, Akida." His smile was infectious as he too reached out for my hand before turning his smooth brown eyes toward Arabella. He bowed his head slightly, respect in his stance as he grabbed her hand, placing a gentle kiss on her knuckles.

Akida and I had been on a handful of assignments for the Spiral together, some of which required us to spend several long nights together in shitty hotels. So, we knew each other pretty well. And he had been more of a playboy than I had, dancing through women like he was changing his clothes. The fact that he was also incredibly attractive was a huge help and had me instinctively tightening my arm around Arabella's waist.

"And who is this?" he asked, a smile cracking across his face.

"This is my wife, Arabella Stark." His eyes went wide, an

apologetic look crossing his face as he looked back and forth between us.

"I did not know you were married," a woman's voice echoed down the stone hallway. "It seems I've missed quite a bit during my time away." A moment later Lucia Cuervo rounded the corner with her eldest son, Mateo, close behind. Despite her small stature, even with the 6-inch heels she wore, she barreled through the large men in front of her, her deep red manicured fingers reaching out to pull my face down toward hers. I kept my arm around Arabella as Lucia kissed both my cheeks before turning her amber eyes on my wife. "I am Lucia Cuervo. It's so nice to meet you."

Her smile was huge as she looked Arabella up and down before pulling her into a tight hug. She stiffened but only for a moment before forcing her arms around the other woman as she greeted her the same. Mateo, who was barely 18 and newly appointed as the second council member for the Cuervo family, looked flustered as he stood behind his mother. Donning a gray suit that was 2 sizes too big for him, he was awkwardly running his hand through his thick brown hair as his eyes passed back and forth between the back of his mother's head and the rest of us standing there. I was about to speak, to try and relieve the kid of the anxiety that I could see building up in his young features, but Arabella beat me to it.

"If it makes you feel any better," she said, her voice sweet. "I'm probably more unprepared for this council meeting than you are." She smiled at him, and I watched the deep blush that painted his chestnut cheeks as his hand moved to rub the back of his neck.

"It's that obvious, huh?" he asked, his tone trying to sound playful. "I thought I was playing it pretty cool." Lucia's eyes went wide before they landed back on mine, and I could sense her words without her speaking. Those were the first words Mateo had ever said to anyone outside of those he trusted. Having seen his father being viciously torn apart by Fiends, he had closed himself off from pretty much the rest of the word. I had suggested making him a part of the council in the hopes that he'd open up to at least one of us. And of all of those it could have been, it made sense that it would be the one that also thought she was broken. Lucia grabbed Arabella in a hug again, the tears floating at the back of her eyes as she spoke.

"I think I may be in love with your wife, Keiran." Arabella looked up at me, her brow slanted in confusion. I hooked my arm around her waist again as Lucia turned her attention to Kijani, her voice rising an octave higher, and her highlighted brown hair pulled back in a tight ponytail bounced animatedly as they spoke about the possibility of Mateo joining Akida on an upcoming assignment.

"What was that about?" Arabella asked, her voice low so that only I could hear her.

"I'll tell you about it later," I said, placing a gentle kiss on her forehead.

"Get a room." Her high-pitched tone was filled with amusement as Mei Chen accompanied by her daughter Li joined us as well. Mei's smile was devious as her coffee brown eyes passed between Arabella and I before landing on the lacy fabric poking out from my suit pocket.

"New handkerchief?" she asked, her perfect eyebrow lifting in accusation.

"My favorite one," I said with a large grin. Arabella groaned, covering her face with her hands in embarrassment.

"Forgive her," Li said, holding her heavily tattooed hand out toward Arabella. "She has zero filter." Arabella, redder than I had ever seen her, gripped her hand back. "Makes it really hard to bring a girl home sometimes. I'm Li, by the way. This is my mother, Mei."

"Nonsense," Mei defended. "I'm a delight to be around.

Maybe that pantsuit you are wearing is making you so uptight." Li's laughter joined her mother's as everyone started to gravitate toward the table, taking their seats across from one another. Arabella turned toward me, elbowing me in the side.

"That's a horrible first impression of me," she said, venom lining her hushed voice. "That's humiliating!" I was still smiling as I spun around, my arm pulling her with me. I dipped my head down so that I could whisper in her ear.

"As far as I'm concerned, they should be happy I'm not bending you over this table and fucking you in front of them." She stiffened, her eyes going wide as she looked up at me and I couldn't help the laugh that left me. She really was fucking gorgeous when she was turned on, especially when she was trying to hide it. I moved my hand to her lower back, guiding her toward the chair that was sitting to the right of the head of the table.

Normally, I'd have my second on the opposite end to ensure that we were covered at both sides. Since there were no surviving members of the Stark family other than myself and Alexander, who had disappeared from our way of life just before Elizabeth died, Emery was usually the one to step in as my second. But she was more than willing to give up the seat when I told her that Arabella was going to take that place. But I didn't trust Malachi, so I wanted her close to me until I learned what his game plan was. Kijani sat in front of her, his large hands folded together as they rested on the table.

He sighed, "Leave it to Malachi to ask for a meeting that he is late to."

CHAPTER THIRTY-ONE

Arabella

"It's a powerplay," Keiran said as he leaned forward with his elbows on the table. The simple movement shouldn't have been as sexy as it was but here I was, my mind going to very inappropriate places instead of how much this was probably going to suck. "He's done it ever since I took his place as Proctor. It doesn't bother me nearly as much as he thinks it does." The others laughed, such a glaring disparity between the way council meetings with my father had gone and the way they were reacting with each other now. The members now were not the same as those who held these seats when my father had been in charge and part of me wondered if that was intentional on Keiran's part. Maybe that was also why he had placed the extra security lock on the door.

But beyond that, the way every one of them had greeted him with zero animosity was different as well. And the way he greeted them with equal respect. They looked at him like a true leader and the thought made me smile. It fell just as quickly though, when the energy in the room shifted, a deep seeded feeling of dread washing over me. Before I could brace myself for the pit forming in my stomach, Avery walked into the room, the pale pink dress she wore, slinking slowly behind her. The arrogant smile that painted her face deepened when she met my gaze, my obvious nerves dancing behind my expression. Her smile seemed to falter, though, when she realized that I was sitting right next to Keiran, something I'm sure she was used to doing and I hated that the thought made me uncomfortable.

I watched as she took the seat next to Mateo, who squirmed uncomfortably under her scrutiny. I knew that look of disgust all too well. Poor guy. I tore my eyes away from the way his shaky fingers pulled nervously at themselves as we heard his voice before he entered the room.

"Do excuse us for being late," Malachi said, his tone and energy as arrogant as I remembered. He looked older, the fine lines becoming more prominent around his permanent frown and the grey sprinkled throughout his dark blonde hair. The grey suit he wore was slightly too big for him, as if he had recently lost some weight and his hands seemed almost frail as he took his place in the lone seat on the opposite end of Keiran's. If I had known any better it was like he was only a fraction of what he once was, like this couldn't possibly be the man that had broken me worse than any of the others. But as his stare moved to me, those eyes full of disdain never leaving mine, I knew very well this was the same man. "Arabella."

"Malachi." My tone was just as emotionless as his. I wasn't going to allow this man to see the turmoil that he still awoke in me. He opened his mouth to speak, venomous words on the tip of his tongue before Keiran cut him off.

"Now that the Blackwoods have decided to grace us with their presence, we should get started." Malachi's lips slammed shut, irritation on his face. He never would have just shut up if someone had spoken to him like that. Especially someone who was younger than he was and the thought of how this change in dynamics came about, again crossed my mind. "The first topic I'd like to discuss is revenue." Kijani spoke first.

"Since Necro attacks have decreased by a very large amount, most of our revenue is coming from our own personal avenues or whatever assignments the Spiral may offer."

"Has there been a decrease in your profits though?" Keiran asked. Kijani shook his head with a laugh.

"Akida is quite good with people, especially the ladies." Kijani's smile was broad, his pride for his son's strength written on his face. I could tell that Akida had been a flirt the moment he flashed that pearly white smile at me and kissed my hand. I knew that same greeting had probably gotten him lucky on more than one occasion. "The real estate business has been better than ever."

"For us as well," Li offered. Despite the light tone in her voice, Li's face remained stoic, her slicked back black hair pulling together the rest of her chic vibe. I just knew that she had seen things that caused that hardened expression. Her mahogany eyes crinkled in excitement though as she tapped her tattooed fingers against the table in an even rhythm. "We just signed a deal for a large shipment of fruit with a local farm. The brewery has been trying to expand to new flavors. We recently released a strawberry peach fusion wine that is truly divine."

"And how has the restaurant been fairing, Mateo?" His eyes went wide as Keiran mentioned him directly, instead of his mother. Mateo sat up straight, his words coming out uneven.

"I-uh- it's okay. I think. We made 3 times the profit of last year." Lucia chimed in, and I watched Mateo's shoulders physically relax.

"We've opted for delivery as well now," she said. "With the colder months coming, people will still be able to enjoy 5-star dining without having to leave the comfort of their homes."

"That's great to hear," Keiran replied. His friendly demeanor changed though as he lifted his gaze toward my father, who had been watching me the whole time, his hatred spewing toward me from across the table. "And the hotel? I am hoping there hasn't been another incident since you upped security?"

"An unfortunate incident," Malachi said, dragging his eyes away from me to look back at Keiran. "That entire floor is still down for renovation to remove the blood of that poor young woman." I turned toward Keiran in question, but he just shook his head and I'd figured he'd tell me later.

"Apart from that one, there hasn't been another Fiend attack since you've opened the club," Avery said, her face as unfriendly as Malachi's.

"They seem to crave sex, power, and the worst parts of humanity over simply wanting blood. It seems the club is serving its purpose then to keep them away from humans as much as possible. At least the ones that don't want to be consumed." I had wondered why Keiran had allowed those vile things to occupy the space of the club. I had questioned whether he loosened his resolve when it came to fighting demons, but I guess it was another way in which I doubted who he really was. I felt a sense of guilt as I reached for his hand under the table. He seemed taken aback but gripped my hand in his before continuing. "Hopefully it will keep them occupied until we can figure out where they are coming from."

"I think that it has something to do with the Spider," I said, and all eyes moved to me, making me somewhat nervous. But the adoration in Keiran's eyes as he met mine made me continue. "I don't really have much to go on, but I haven't seen a single Necro since I've been back. When we went to that party, there were over a dozen of them just standing there, like they were waiting for him to give them the go ahead."

"Necros purely go after blood," Mei said, her voice filled

with concern as she picked an invisible piece of lint from her white sequined dress. "No one can control one of those things." I nodded.

"My point exactly. I think he has something to do with it. I just don't know what yet."

"Then perhaps you should keep baseless accusations to yourself," Malachi said. "The gods know you are too impulsive."

"Watch your fucking tongue," Keiran snapped. Malachi pressed his lips, crossing his arms over his chest defensively.

"It is true," he sneered. "You can't just walk in here after years of abandoning your duty as a Mercenary and have a say that holds merit. Which, by the way, if we are finished with the formalities, I'd like to discuss the whole reason I asked for this meeting. Arabella must be punished for killing Damian Stark." The words spilled from his mouth like he had been struggling to hold them in.

"Her statement does hold merit," Li said, her voice just as cruel as Malachi's. "It can't just be a coincidence that more Fiends have been showing up since the Spider came into town. He is very much a person of interest, even if he is a member of the Spiral. And secondly, Arabella did us all a favor by killing Damian Stark. He was just as cruel and vile as his father and caused more problems than he helped."

"I think that she has punished herself enough for what happened," Keiran added. "And you have punished her enough in her lifetime for what you think she did wrong." Malachi's hands landed hard on the table, the sound making me jump.

"She was an insolent brat that needed to be taught that she can't always get her way. And it seems she needs to be reminded again that she cannot just disappear and abandon her responsibility to this family. As the head of the Blackwood family, her punishment gets decided by me whether you agree with it or not, Keiran." Keiran never took his eyes off my father as he lifted his eyebrow in amusement.

"Actually," he said, an edge in his voice, "I do get a say. She is no longer a Blackwood." Avery finally looked up from the spot on the table that her eyes had settled the moment Malachi started talking.

"What are you talking about?" The smile that spread across Keiran's face was unhinged.

"Not only is she a Stark, but she is also the wife of the Proctor. Which means she outranks even you, Malachi." Avery's jaw dropped, the shock swirling around in her angry eyes.

"Since when?" she shrieked.

"About an hour ago," I admitted, a smile on my face at her reaction.

"Oh, remind me to send a wedding gift to the club later so I do not forget," Lucia said with humor in her voice as she patted my hand, and I had never wanted to hug another person so badly before.

"It still sets the precedent that one would get away with such stupidity if there are no consequences," Malachi seethed.

"If you insult my wife one more time, I will be more than happy to show you the consequences of such stupidity." Keiran's tone was calm but laced with the promise of violence. Malachi's aggressive gaze passed between the both of us before he finally turned to me, his face as cruel as I remembered when he'd punish me.

"I wonder," he said bitterly, "If you'd still feel so proud if you knew that everything that happened had been for nothing." I looked at him strangely.

"What does that mean?" He smiled, the action vicious and unnatural.

"You ran away because you were so sure that he had picked Avery." Avery shot a glance toward him in warning. "I want to know how you feel when you find out that it was never what you thought it was."

"Shut up," Avery snapped, panic in her eyes. His smile only broadened.

"I've had enough of you speaking in riddles, Malachi," Keiran retorted. He started laughing.

"Go ahead, Avery. Tell them the truth." All eyes were now on her. Her breath quickened the longer she hesitated.

"Speak." That one word was filled with such anger as it left Keiran's mouth. Avery looked down at her hands before she finally said something.

"We never slept together." Her voice was so low, I had to strain to hear what she had said. "I faked it." I felt like my lungs collapsed as I pulled my hand away from Keiran's to grip my chest. "Keiran was super drunk when he stumbled into our front door. He kept saying that he needed to fix it, that he needed to tell Arabella that he was stupid and sorry for what he said." I felt Keiran stiffen beside me, like he too was fighting to keep it together. "I tried to talk him out of it," she continued, more conviction in her tone the longer she spoke. "He was sitting on the sofa when he got a text from Arabella."

Memories from that night filled my head. Going to Keiran's place but he wasn't there and texting him to ask him where he was. I remembered the text perfectly. **Where are you? This is a stupid fight and I want you crawling on your knees to beg for my forgiveness**. There was even a laughing emoji at the end of it. His reply was even quick, and I thought maybe he had been waiting for it.

"I grabbed his phone and sent a message back saying that he was at the Blackwood house. Once I saw that you had read it, I deleted the conversation so he wouldn't know. Not even 5 minutes later I saw the lights from your car pull into the driveway." Avery finally lifted her eyes to mine, like she wanted me to know how much she enjoyed what she did. "Keiran had passed out on the couch, so I unbuckled his belt and got on his lap. I even dropped my underwear on the ground first and started to moan to really make you think that we were having sex." I had to grip the table, a slew of emotions ripping their way through my body.

When I finally caught my breath, I said, "D- do you really hate me that much?"

Angrily, she yelled, "I was fucking perfect! In everything I did and still all he ever cared about was making you a fucking weapon! I wanted you to feel the betrayal I felt." When I realized the truth behind those words, my face grew cold. The betrayal that she spoke of was in her father caring more about making a weapon out of me, the little girl that wasn't even his, than he did about his own flesh and blood.

"You are so desperate for daddy's approval," I spat, "that you refuse to see that the problem was in him. Never in you or I. It's sad." My voice grew harsher. "It's pathetic and I feel sorry for you, Avery." As I said her name, she held her head high, her lips pressed together in an attempt at pride.

"I've heard enough," Keiran finally spoke, malice in his voice. "This council meeting is over. Everyone but the Blackwoods may leave." He stared down at Avery as she squirmed under his intense gaze. There was shame hidden in her expression, but I knew she would never admit it. The others spoke their goodbyes and congratulations quickly as they hurried out of the council room. Not that I blamed them. The tension was palpable. But as I looked to Malachi, his face still twisted in amusement at the chaos he just caused, I had a newfound hatred for that man.

"I hate you," I said.

CHAPTER THIRTY-TWO

Keiran

"Your words mean nothing to me," Malachi scoffed. I looked down at her to see the tears dancing at the back of her eyes, refusing to show this man any vulnerability. Denying him the satisfaction of seeing him break her again and I've never felt more anger than I had at that moment. I lifted my hand under her chin, tilting her face toward mine and away from the people that have done nothing but torture her at every chance they got. I had to swallow back my own emotion as I watched her lower lip quiver.

"Go wait for me outside," I said, my voice soft. She knit her eyebrows together, so I smiled and kissed her forehead. "It's okay. I'll be behind you shortly." She hesitated but did as I said, not making a single glance back at the three of us before she walked out. I turned back to Malachi, any semblance or nicety gone from my demeanor. "Do you have any idea the lengths that woman would go for those that she cares about?"

He sighed, "She is nothing but a spoiled brat." Losing

what little control I had over my temper, I slammed my fists down on the table, making Avery jump.

"Watch your fucking tongue. She was your fucking daughter and the only reason you told us the truth was because you wanted to hurt her." He shook his head, and I dug my fingers into the palm of my hand to keep myself from leaping across the table at him. To keep from beating that arrogant smirk off of his face.

"No, she was my fucking weapon. She would have died if it were not for me."

"A weapon that has 20 years of pent-up rage mixed in with that power that you so desperately want. Because let's be honest, Malachi. That's the real reason you are angry. You're angry because you can't have that power for yourself. You're too weak." There was a satisfaction in the way his nostrils flared at my words.

"What did you say to me?"

"You're too weak," I repeated. "You were too weak to fight against me for the position of Proctor. You were too weak to keep your family in power and Jezebel had to come beg me to help you. And you are too weak to have the power that you so desperately want. I will not allow you to continue to hurt my wife because you're a pathetic excuse of a man." I stood, readjusting my suit jacket as I walked to stand beside the two of them, looking down at them in disgust. "The two of you are removed from this council. Jezebel will take your place because I have respect for that woman and will not allow your actions to affect her as well." I lifted my gaze toward the entrance, not allowing them another glance. "Should either of you end up in the presence of Arabella Stark again, whatever happens will be entirely up to her. Now get out of my fucking council room."

After staying behind to ensure they left, I found my beautiful bride waiting in the car. She said nothing as I got in and we drove off. Her face was emotionless as she kept her eyes forward and I wondered what storm was thrashing around in her beautiful mind.

"Well, I'm pretty sure they forgot about your underwear in my pocket after that," I chuckled as I looked at her, almost ready to plead with her to get her to say something. All I got was a halfhearted smile. I reached over and grabbed her hand, pulling it over to kiss her fingers. "Are you okay?" She looked at me for a quick moment as she just nodded her head. "Please say something." She opened her mouth but snapped it shut and that bottom lip fucking quivered again as a single tear slid down her cheek. She turned her head away, looking toward the passing buildings through the window to hide her face. "Hey. Look at me." She shook her head again before a heart wrenching sob filled the space between us. I nearly caused an accident as I pulled to the side of the road, throwing the car into park so I could grab her. I cupped her face, turning it so that she would look at me. Those green eyes were haunting when they met mine, their color even more vibrant when she cried. It was heartbreakingly beautiful. "Please," I pleaded as she dropped them away from me. Slowly, she raised her gaze to mine again, tears drying on her cheeks as she tried to fight back her sadness. "It changes nothing."

I knew Malachi's words were tossing around in her head. It was all for nothing. He chose those words because he knew what she would do to herself when Avery told the truth. She would doubt every decision she had made and blame herself for the outcome.

"I feel like it changes everything," she said, her voice cracking at the end. "All of that time lost." She pulled away from me. "Everything that you went through because I thought you chose her over me. The shame I carried for feeling that way. The way that I treated you, Keiran. It wasn't fair to you." I pulled her back to me, grabbing her face again so I could wipe her tears away with my thumbs.

"Nor was it fair to you, Arabella," I said, my own voice sounding uneven as she closed her eyes. "But the only thing that is different is that I will be able to look in the mirror and not hate myself for what I thought I did to you." She looked up at me again, a fresh set of tears spilling out over her lower lashes. I pressed my forehead to hers like I was trying to pull the sadness from her into myself. "There is nothing we can do about the way it happened." I pulled back to look at her, a small smile on my face. "All we can do is remind each other that we aren't alone anymore." I used the same words she had said to me when I thought the whole world was against me. The same words that brought me back from the edge, time and time again. She took a deep breath, broken by a small hiccup at the end, as she stared at me so intensely it almost made me pull away.

"I love you." The words were so quiet I almost missed it. I leaned back in my seat, my mind going haywire. Sure, she had told me that she was in love with me. But hearing those 3 words leave her lips was a euphoric feeling. I had never done drugs, but I assumed this was what it felt like. She turned beat red, quickly turning in her seat so she was facing forward. "Sorry. It just kind of slipped out." I reached over and grabbed her, pulling her onto my lap with a startling force. Her eyes went big, but she melted into me as soon as I kissed her.

"I love you," I said against her lips. Her hands found their way to the back of my head, pulling me further into her mouth as my hands moved down her body, settling around the back of her thighs. She moaned into my mouth, making my dick spring to life again when I thought about how she wasn't wearing anything underneath. I broke away from her, our breaths fast and staggered. "We need to go home." Her smile was mischievous as she sat back in my lap, moving her hips slowly so she could grind against my ever-growing cock. My hands moved to grip her perfect ass and keep her still. "Unless you want others to hear you screaming my name, we need to leave."

CHAPTER THIRTY-THREE

Arabella

My body felt like I had been awake and moving for a week straight. I hated crying. But more importantly, I hated that once again the people that had been the only family I had ever known were the reason behind it. Avery's truth had broken me more than I was ever going to admit. But I had blindly believed that Keiran chose to abandon me the way they had despite knowing who he really was, with or without that stupid fight. So, I couldn't just blame them. The life that I had thrust myself into was entirely my doing and like he had said, there was no changing that. And of course, the fucker would use my own words against me.

"Can I ask you something?" I said as he drove back to the apartment.

"Always."

"Why did Lucia look like she was going to cry when I was talking to Mateo?"

"He doesn't talk to very many people," he admitted. "After his father was killed in front of him, he kind of just shut himself off from almost everyone. I suggested making him a council member because I had hoped that it would help him open up to one of us. He never speaks at the meetings though so when he spoke to you, it took her by surprise."

"And what about you?" He kept telling me that I had this habit of making myself seem small and insignificant. Which, valid point. But he had this habit of suppressing everything he deemed as unnecessary and actively sought out how to heal those things in others. He knit his eyebrows together as he looked back and forth between me and the road. "Were you ever able to open up to one of them when you needed it?" He was quiet for a long time, and I thought he wasn't going to answer.

"I suppose I tried," he answered honestly. "During assignments with Akida, there were times when we'd speak about past experiences."

"I feel like there is a but at the end of that statement." I watched as his hand moved to the back of his neck, rubbing it roughly as he cracked it from side to side.

"I couldn't be honest about it." He paused before continuing. "I couldn't tell him that the lives that we took meant far less to me than they did to him. That when I was drenched in the blood of those I was sent to kill, I relished in it because that was the only time that I could feel something anymore." I felt my heart shatter because I knew that he meant that with everything he had. "So, when you told me that you didn't feel bad for killing Damian, I understood more than you think I do."

"You remembered that you had feelings again," I said, repeating with a mocking tone what Emery had so blatantly spoken the other night. He grinned.

"No, I realized I had feelings again when you pushed by me in the diner and told me to fuck off."

"Maybe you have a degradation kink," I joked. He laughed, a full belly laugh for the first time since we were younger. "You should do that more often."

"Do what?"

"That laugh. It was pretty sexy."

"Yeah?" His voice had dropped lower, that same aroused tone that he had earlier when he mentioned me screaming his name... "What are you thinking about?" I hadn't realized that I had grown quiet, my eyes focusing on the fact that he still had a hard on from when I so boldly was going to let him fuck me in his car right there in the middle of town. He reached over and gripped my upper thigh, his fingers brushing dangerously close to where I wanted him and my breath hitched. He chuckled, perfectly aware of the way my body craved his touch.

"How taxes are outrageous, and Capitalism will be the downfall of humanity," I said, the sarcasm thick as I answered his question. "You know, the trivial stuff." I waved my hand dismissively with a smirk. He lifted an eyebrow and ran his tongue along his bottom lip. Fuck, how much longer was this drive going to take?

I asked myself that question but as soon as he whipped the car into the carpark of the apartment building, that boldness seemed to be replaced with nerves. I desperately wanted this man, but I was woefully aware that I didn't have a whole lot of experience. I'd been with 2 other people. One was the guy I lost my virginity to back when I was 18 just to get it over with. It lasted less than two minutes and I broke up with the guy as soon as it was over. The other had been a guy that had also unfortunately found himself working for Alexander. We had messed around a few times when I was craving physical touch until he had gotten himself killed by our boss. Even then, it wasn't like he knew how to get a woman off. I mean, back in the council room was the first time I had ever had an orgasm that didn't come from myself. I was about to be putty in this man's hands.

I could feel the electric charge between us as we walked into the building, his hand resting on my lower back. I thought I was going to jump out of my skin when he opened the door and I pushed my way inside. Emery and Sakura had already left, though the clothing bags and their contents were still splayed across the sofa. I sighed.

"This place is a mess. I should clean up." His arm was around my waist quickly, his voice in my ear.

"Leave it." I melted against him, my head leaning back against his chest as he bent further down to kiss my neck. "Are you nervous?"

"I want you," I replied, my voice shaky. He spun me around, his hands sliding down my body to the back of my thighs. He lifted me up and I wrapped my legs around his waist.

"That doesn't answer my question, Arabella." I bit down hard on my lip, his eyes watching the movement with pure hunger in them. Keeping one hand holding me up, he used the other to pull it from my grasp before he kissed me. I whimpered against his lips when his free hand then worked to undo the zipper on the back of my dress. He pulled his mouth from mine. "Are you nervous?" He wouldn't ask a third time.

"Yes," I whispered. He sat me down on the edge of the bed, and I hadn't realized that he had been moving toward the bedroom the whole time he had kissed me. He stood between my legs as his fingers started to work on the buttons of his shirt. My eyes went wide before he put his finger under my chin, forcing me to look up at him.

"Why?" he asked as he continued with the buttons. My pulse quickened as I tried to keep my eyes on his, though my hands had a mind of their own as they moved to unbuckle his belt. His laugh was deep and sexy.

"Because I just want to be good enough," I said finally. His hands stilled on the last button, and I couldn't help it as my eyes dipped lower, running along the length of his bare muscular chest. And there, just above his right pectoral muscle, was an engraved blue spiral. I absently traced it with my finger, that ever-present guilt settling deep inside my stomach. I couldn't fathom the things he had done because of that symbol. Because of me and my decisions. His thumb pressed against my pinched brow, smoothing its surface as he spoke.

"It changes nothing," he said, reiterating his earlier declaration that what they had done didn't change the way we felt. I felt my lip wobble as I tried to fight off the heavy feeling in my chest. In one quick motion, my back was on the bed. Keiran hovered above me as he slid my dress off with more ease than I would have done myself, leaving me lying there completely naked. He sat back on his heels, his eyes roaming over me possessively and I instinctively covered myself, my cheeks flushing with warmth. He grabbed my hands, resting them on my flat stomach as he shook his head. "You are good enough, Arabella." His face turned devious though as he moved above me again, this time pinning my arms above my head. I squirmed underneath him, my need so strong it was overwhelming as he kissed me aggressively. "If you try to cover yourself up again, I will not let you come." My eyes went wide. "Do you understand?" I nodded; my voice nonexistent. "Say you understand."

"I understand," I forced out. He grinned as he stood up from the bed again, his eyes raking slowly over my body once more in admiration as he licked his lips.

"You're so fucking beautiful." I wanted to hide my face and it took all of my restraint to keep my arms at my side. To help, I focused on his large hands as they pulled his belt off the rest of the way, dropping to the ground with a sound that seemed to echo in my brain. There was zero hesitation in his movements as he undid his fly and freed himself from the rest of his clothing. I was almost jealous how comfortable he was in his own body. Naturally, my gaze dipped lower, admiring every sculpted inch of his chest, his thighs, that V shaped muscle just before stopping at his midsection... And holy fucking shit, I felt all the breath leave my lungs.

I knew he had a big dick. I could tell with the way it strained in his pants and pressed against me earlier. But seeing it had my mouth popping open in shock. I didn't even think I'd be able to wrap my hand around it... A dip in the bed pulled my thoughts back to him as he pushed my knees apart with his hips, his hands moving back to pin mine above our heads again. My body bowed against him like it was commanded to do so which made a low chuckle escape his lips as they hovered above mine.

"I love how responsive your body is to me," he said, his breath warm against my face. He kissed me passionately, his tongue exploring my mouth with vigor and possession. My legs wrapped around his waist, pulling him tighter against me and I moaned into his mouth when the underside of his cock pressed against my core. I ground my hips against him, silently begging this man to give me the release my body wanted. "Patience, baby girl. I've waited a long time to be able to worship your body." As he said it, his lips trailed down my jaw and neck, the longing in them burning my flesh as they went. He let go of my hands, his own running down my body like he was studying it, learning an ancient language written on my skin that only he could decipher. They settled at my breasts, his large fingers making them seem small in his grasp, at the same time as he sucked one of them into his mouth.

"Keiran," I moaned, my body jumping at the electricity his touch emitted. He groaned, the vibration of it making me pant as his tongue swirled around my pebbled nipple.

"I would definitely kill Sakura over these," he said before slowly moving to the other breast to repeat the same process. Even though I thought I was going to come out of my own skin, I giggled. I felt his smile as his mouth continued its exploration, placing gentle deliberate kisses down the valley between my breasts and down my stomach. "Open your eyes." I hadn't realized that they had closed until I looked down to see him hovering between my legs, his mouth just above my clit and his eyes on my face. "I want you to watch me taste you. And remember, do not cover your face."

CHAPTER THIRTY-FOUR

I didn't even have time to respond to him as his tongue dipped inside of my pussy and my ass came up off the bed. I cried out, a sound that didn't even sound like me spilling from my lips like it was calling to him as my fingers gripped the sheets.

"I thought I was going to have to work you up a little more," he said, humor in his voice before his tongue brushed against my clit again. He'd go back and forth between licking and sucking, driving me wild. "You're already so wet for me." Lick. "So ready for my cock." Suck.

"P-p." Was that even a real fucking sound that came out of my mouth?

"Can you repeat that?" His tone was still joking.

"Please," I pleaded, slightly remembering that I knew how to speak.

"Please what, baby?" I let out a frustrated sigh. I could barely register a thought in my brain, let alone form actual fucking words to tell this man what I desperately wanted more than anything right now was to be wrapped around him.

"I- I want." I shook my head. "I need-" Fuck, what was I

trying to say? I watched him as he pushed himself upward so he could sit back on his heels, my eyes leaving his for a moment to watch the way his huge erection bobbed between us. He gripped my ankle, pulling it forward to rest on his shoulder before grabbing one of the pillows above us and sliding it underneath my back. The whole time, he kept his eyes on my face, that fucking cocky grin never leaving his as he spoke.

"Is this what you want, Arabella?" He gripped the base of his cock, my eyes hungrily watching the way he stroked it. "-what you need?" Still holding onto it, he pressed his large head against my core, slowly sliding it back and forth to coat himself in my arousal. My moan was muffled by the growl that left his chest. Glad I wasn't the only one losing it here.

"I need you, Keiran," I panted. I watched the patience he seemed to have dim considerably as he positioned his head at my opening. The lust in this man's eyes was fucking unholy as he pushed forward, just the tip of his cock sinking inside of me. My back arched, my hands moving to press against his lower abdomen as my head fell back against the bed. He gripped my thigh as he pulled out and then slid back in slowly, pushing another inch further. I felt my body straining to stretch around him as he repeated the movement, pushing further in with each thrust.

"Fuck," he groaned, his deep sex filled voice even hotter than his normal one as he pressed his lips against my ankle. He'd pause after each thrust, allowing my body to fully stretch for him. I had never felt so full before and just when I think that was as far as he could go, he'd go deeper.

"Holy fuck, Keiran," I whimpered, my nails dragging down his abs as I rolled my hips in rhythm with his.

"I know, baby. You're almost there. You're doing so good." If it wasn't his large head rubbing against that sweet spot with each thrust, his fucking words of affirmation were going to be my undoing. I felt the tension building low in my belly already as his movements quickened, the sounds of our heavy breaths growing louder and more desperate. I tried to hold out, to push down the overwhelming tension that was building but I knew I was losing the battle by a landslide. As if he could sense it, Keiran's hand pressed down on my lower abdomen, making my need for release even more intense. "Let me see you come undone, Arabella." Like my body was waiting for his permission, I cried out, my orgasm ripping through me with such force that I thought I was dying. Keiran's hips slowed as my body convulsed around his cock and the intensity had tears prickling at the back of my eyes. "Such a good girl," he muttered as he dropped my ankle back down on the bed.

Giving me no time to tense up, he hooked his arm under my knee, flipping me over so that I was on all fours. With more force than before, he slammed into me from behind and it felt like he had hit the back of my teeth. He had definitely been holding back. I pushed back against him, earning a deep animalistic sound from him as he gripped my hips. I dropped my head, my moan ringing in my ears as he picked up rhythm again.

"You take my cock so well, baby," he groaned, his voice tense like he was losing a battle of his own. My body bowed and he moved one hand to press down on the middle of my back, pushing my backside further up to give him better access. He fucked into me harder, that tingling sensation building again as his cock rubbed against my g spot repeatedly.

"Oh, that feels good," I mewled, my fingers gripping the silk sheets. His fingers entangled in my hair, wrapping it once around his hand before he pulled. Not hard enough to hurt but hard enough that I was at his mercy.

"How good, baby girl?"

"So fucking good." My cries were getting louder, almost pleading.

"You're gonna drive me insane." I could hear the smile in his voice. Without breaking his pace, his other arm wrapped around me. His fingers pressed against my clit, moving in a slow circular motion as he continued to pound into me. I tensed up again, the sensation so intense that I couldn't think straight.

"Keiran!"

"That's right, baby. Cry out for me."

"I'm gonna-" The breath left my lungs, cutting my words off as I reached another orgasm, my pussy clenching onto him like it didn't want to let him go. His fingers continued their assault with more force, dragging out my release.

"Fuck, Arabella," he said, his own voice pleading. He slammed into me one more time before his body stiffened, his cock twitching as he emptied himself into me with a throaty yell.

He stayed positioned inside of me, our connected bodies the only thing keeping me from crumbling down on the bed, as we tried to catch our breath. He gently let go of my hair as he slid out of me, and I winced. I was definitely going to be sore tomorrow. He leaned over me, dipping his head so he could kiss the back of my shoulder.

"Are you okay?" he asked in a gruff voice, his arm sliding around my waist as I nearly fell forward on the bed. I could only nod, my mind stuck on stupid as he plopped down on his back, pulling me with him to lay on his chest. "Are you sure?" Another nod. "Have you forgotten how to speak?" Another nod. His chest shook with laughter, and I found it soothing as I traced my finger across it in a figure 8 motion. His arm tightened around me as he pressed a kiss to the top of my head. "I love you." I moved my head up to look at him, resting my chin on top of my hand and smiled mischievously.

"I can't tell you that right now." He lifted an eyebrow.

"Why not?"

"Because I don't know if I'd say it because I meant it or if I'd say it because I'm delirious from the best sex I've ever had." His laugh was genuine before he flipped us over again so that he was on top of me, pinning my arms above my head once more. He kissed me quickly before pulling back to look in my eyes.

"Oh, baby," he said, his husky voice taunting, "I'm not even close to being done with you yet."

CHAPTER THIRTY-FIVE

Keiran

I wasn't sure what time it was by the time my eyes rolled open. By how bright the sun was shining through a crack of the blackout curtains, it was well into the morning, possibly into the afternoon when I awoke. My arms felt empty and for a moment my brain had convinced me that last night had been a dream that ended with Arabella falling asleep naked in my arms. I fought off a solemn feeling in my chest until a delicious aroma filled my nose and pulled me out of the bed.

In case my brain had been playing tricks on me and I was about to find Emery or Sakura cooking in the apartment, I slid into a pair of sweats and made my way out to the kitchen. There I found her, though, wearing nothing but a thin shirt of mine that fell around her beautiful thighs as she stood at the stove with her back toward me. Even then she was breathtaking, and I had to just stand there and watch her. She wiggled that juicy little ass of hers, dancing to a beat that must have been in her head, and I bit back a laugh so I wouldn't make my presence known. I wanted to see her like this a little bit longer. I wanted to see her when her guard wasn't up. But as she clenched her thighs, a small groan leaving her lips, I felt a little guilty.

Guilty because every time I touched her, every time I'd see that look in her eyes right after I finished fucking her into oblivion, all I could think about was how we could have had this a long time ago. We probably would have had a child by now. Or a few because I couldn't get enough of her. It would make me hate the Blackwoods even more and in return, I'd fuck her harder like my cock was trying to make up for the years we'd missed. In our bed. On the ground. Against the wall. In the shower. I was unrelenting until she passed out from the sheer exhaustion last night. She was undoubtedly sore this morning. I probably should have given her a break. But when the sound of a spatula hitting the floor resounded through the space and she bent down to pick it up, putting on display her ass and that pretty little pussy of hers, my cock rose to attention, and I groaned in admiration at the beauty of her. At my sound, she snapped upright, whipping around to face me.

"Can I make a request for you to always walk around in nothing but my shirt?" She turned a vibrant red but rolled her eyes.

"Shut up." She turned back around, focusing her attention back on the food she was cooking. I closed the distance between us to grab her by the waist and pull her back against me. I moved my head down to kiss down her neck and shoulder blade. "You're distracting me." Her voice was shaky, the arousal in her tone making me harder.

"Hm," I muttered, moving my lips to her ear. "Am I?" My hand moved under the shirt, my fingers gently brushing against her skin as I trailed them up to her breasts. I grabbed one, gently tugging her stiffened nipple between my fingertips. A quiet moan left her lungs as she pushed into my touch.

"I'm trying to make breakfast," she uttered, clearly on the losing end of this battle for control.

"It does look and smell delicious," I mused. My hand

moved down between her legs as I cupped her pussy and she was already soaked, her arousal coating my fingers as I dipped them inside of her. "But I think I'd like to eat you for breakfast instead."

I was about to reach over and turn the stove off so I could sit her ass on this countertop and lick her clean when my fucking phone started ringing. I wanted to ignore it as I spun her around and was about to drop to my knees and make this woman see stars, but she stopped me.

"It's been ringing all morning," she said, her voice sounding as disappointed as I felt. "It's probably not the best idea to ignore your duties for sex." I lifted a brow in amusement, but my tone was deathly serious as I spoke.

"One of these days I'm going to have you on your knees, sucking my cock after I've been buried inside of you and then you can see why I'd let the world burn for a taste of you." Her eyes went wide as she choked on the breath she sucked in. I was laughing as I walked away from her to grab the stupid fucking device before returning to the living room. It was still fucking ringing, the bastard not allowing me any solace as I answered. "This better be fucking important, Liam."

"Sorry, boss," he said, guilt in his tone. I plopped down on the sofa, leaning forward on my knees as he spoke. "I just wanted to report back some information that I thought would be helpful." I had momentarily forgotten that I had asked Liam to do some digging last night. At some point between the tantric sex, I'd sent him a text asking him to trail Malachi and Avery. I didn't trust them. The way they so casually dropped their entire facade from the last five years just to hurt her seemed like quite a gamble. What was the point? "Avery came poking around the club last night. Said that you had sent her to your office to grab some file that you had been working on for the Spider." I knew she had been hiding something. Even before Arabella showed up, Avery had seemed extra on edge. It never sat right with me that the hotel security all happened to have the same night off when that woman was viciously torn apart. I called bullshit the moment it happened, but she swore that it was an accident. Had 'proof' that it was an unfortunate coincidence. But if she was involved with the Spider and he clearly had something to do with the rapid rise of conscious demons spawning left and right, I don't think it was an accident.

"What did you tell her?" I asked as I closed my eyes and leaned back on the sofa with a sigh.

"That it was locked." I should have focused on what he had been saying but when I felt Arabella straddle me, my eyes snapped open to her gorgeous face, a devious little smirk painting her beautiful lips. "She then asked if I knew where the spare key was, but I told her you didn't have one anymore." She kissed me before sliding down my body, her lips trailing down my bare chest and stomach before she was on her knees in front of me. "She seemed pretty antsy though, like she was on a time schedule or something." Her hands moved to pull at my sweats, and I obliged, lifting slightly off the sofa as she slid them down and my fully erect cock sprang forward between us. Her eyes went wide as it did every time she took in the sight of it, like she was constantly thinking that there was no way she'd be able to handle it. Yet she did every time like the good fucking girl that she was.

"Did she leave?" I asked, my eyes focused on Arabella. She positioned herself between my legs before that hypnotic fucking stare moved its focus to my dick again and she licked her lips.

"Yeah. Took a minute though. Emery thought it was weird too. She said she was thinking about trailing her." I had to pull the phone away from my mouth so Liam couldn't hear the moan that left my lips as her hand gripped the base of my cock and she stroked it a couple of times.

"I don't want Emery involved," I breathed, trying to sound angry. Arabella, pleased with my reaction, sat forward on her heels. I had to fight against everything in me as her head dipped lower and she ran her tongue from the base to the head, like she had done with my thumb, before parting her lips around me. "Fuck." She slid me further into her mouth, going until I hit the back of her throat before coming back up and then doing it again. This time as she took me as far back as she could, she swallowed, suctioning the head of my cock in her throat and then sliding back off with a pop.

"I told her that, Keiran," Liam said, completely oblivious to the glorious sight in front of me. I pulled the phone away from my mouth again because the only thing that would make it better...

"Look at me." She did as I said, those fuck me eyes full of tears from choking, meeting mine quickly. "That's my girl." Pinning my phone between my shoulder and my ear, I moved my hands so I could pull the hair back from her face. I wanted to watch how fucking beautiful she looked sucking my cock. "You tell Emery that if she doesn't stay out of it, I will use my authority as Proctor to keep her from doing something stupid." This time I spoke into the phone.

"Will do, boss. I haven't seen Malachi since he left the council meeting though. We all know how vindictive that man is when he doesn't get what he wants." Oh, I did. And he'd be pretty fucking livid if he knew that his revelation didn't do anything and his perfect little weapon was on her knees, salivating like she was fucking starving for me. I started to thrust my hips forward in rhythm with her mouth, nearly coming undone when she swirled her tongue around my head and sucked harder. She moaned, the vibration of it making me twitch in her mouth as my head fell back against the sofa.

"That's exactly why I want him watched." My breathing was quick and if she kept it up, I was going to explode. But I wanted to be buried inside of her for that, her tight little cunt swallowing every fucking drop. "Are you enjoying it, Arabella?" She nodded, keeping the rhythm going as more glorious tears rolled down her face. "Show me." I dropped my head forward and looked down as she moved her hand that had been resting on my thigh and slid it between her legs. She rubbed her fingers inside of her pussy, making me jealous of the movement before they came back up between us, soaking wet.

"I've got others keeping a look out-"

"Liam, I'll call you back." I cut him off and ended the call. I tossed the phone to the side of me, not really caring where it landed. "Stand up." Her mouth slid off with a pop again before she got to her feet, and I pulled her onto my lap. I pulled her lips to mine as she ground against the underside of my erection, coating me in her slickness. She moaned into my mouth before leaning back.

"This was supposed to be about you," she pouted, her lips swollen from being wrapped around me. I scooped my arms under her ass, lifting her up so I could slide my head into her opening. Her eyes lulled shut, her head falling back as I repeated the movement, slowly sliding further inside of her each time I'd move her back down.

"It will always be about you," I groaned. She rocked her hips, swallowing me whole like my cock was fucking made for her. "I'm going to fuck you on every surface of this apartment."

"I fucking hope so," she moaned.

"Fuck, baby," I breathed. In one quick movement, I had her back on the sofa cushion as I wrapped her right leg around my hip. I hooked my arm under the other, pulling it up as I gripped the arm rest and plowed into her.

"Oh yes, Keiran." Hearing my name leave those lips was fucking intoxicating. "Fuck, just like that." She was so close to coming, I could feel it in the way she tightened around me. Good, because my own release was nearing as I pumped into her with so much force her head kept hitting the sofa.

"You feel so fucking good, baby girl." Her back arched, a

loud yell leaving her throat as her fingers dug into my forearms. "And you're all fucking mine."

"I love you." Those three words sent me over the edge at the same time as her body stiffened, her core squeezing every fucking drop of my seed it could as I emptied into her. She lifted her head up and kissed me, her hands moving through my hair possessively and I smiled against her lips.

"I love you, too," I said, out of breath. She giggled as her head fell back down on the cushion. I pulled out, the action making her wince and my face turned guilty. "I'm sorry. I was supposed to give you a break." She shook her head as I sat back on my heels.

"Don't be sorry. It's a good kind of sore." She moved up onto her elbows as she looked up at me. "And I was trying to distract you." Her smile was adorable as I stood up.

CHAPTER THIRTY-SIX

"Distract me from what?" I loved the way her eyes roamed down my naked body hungrily though she blushed when she realized I saw it. I wasn't ashamed of being naked. I had put this body through hell and back to be strong enough to do what needed to be done. I absolutely was not going to be ashamed of that. I just needed to teach her how to be the same. The way she instantly tried to cover herself, the way she always tried to hide her excitement or her embarrassment. It was a habit that needed to be unlearned because no one should feel ashamed by the body they were born with. But even on a purely physical level, she had a killer body. I'd fucking kill someone over those curves.

"Whatever you were talking to Liam about," she said, pulling my mind from the mental image of licking every inch of her. I bent down to scoop her into my arms so I could carry her to the bathroom to clean ourselves up. She wrapped herself around me, her arms and legs locking behind me.

"I wanted him to keep an eye on Malachi and Avery." I hated the way her body went rigid when I said their names. It made me think that I was too nice for what they had done. I sat her down on the bathroom counter and kissed her forehead before turning toward the shower and turning it on.

"Did he find anything?" she asked, her voice saddened. I

walked back to her, forcing her knees on either side of my hips.

"Lift your arms." She instantly did as I said which made me smile. She was actually allowing me to take care of her, allowing herself to let go even if just in small instances. I lifted the shirt up over her head and tossed it onto the counter next to her before lifting her up again to step into the shower. I set her down on her feet and spun her around so that her back was facing me.

"He had said that Avery was acting weird," I continued, reaching around her to grab a washcloth and lather it in soap and hot water.

"Weird how?" Her breath caught when I brushed the cloth against her skin. "I do know how to clean myself, Keiran. I did it myself when we showered last night, too." Her voice sounded annoyed, but I only laughed as I pulled her back against me. She was so stubborn. But like I said, I was worse.

"I'm sure you do," I muttered, wiping the material over her breasts. "But like I said, I want you to trust me enough to let go." She spun around, her eyebrows furrowed in a way that made her look sad.

"I do trust you," she said, a tone of hurt in her voice. I placed my soapy fingers under her chin.

"I know you do, love. But being taken care of is something that you have always struggled with." Her face tightened like she didn't like what I said but then relaxed when she realized that I was right. "I want you to be able to turn that beautiful brain off when you are with me because you know that I will take care of you." She bit down on her lip, her eyes narrowing like she was thinking hard about what I said. After some internal battle in her mind, she turned back around, leaning against my body again.

"How was she acting weird?" she asked again. The satisfied grin never left my face as I focused my hands back on running the washcloth down her body.

"He said that she told him that I sent her there to grab a file I have on the Spider." I felt her body jerk when my hand went between her legs, moving excruciatingly slow as I cleaned one thigh and then the other before brushing against her sex. "I think she may have been involved with him for a while now."

"D-do you think that's why Fiends were able to attack someone at the hotel?" She stammered over her words, trying to keep her breaths even. Like I didn't know the way her body instantly reacted to my touch. And I fucking loved it.

"Yes," I said, pulling my hand away from her thighs. She whimpered, a disappointed sound as I continued with the rest of her body. "They had the roster from that night ready to go before I even knew what officially happened. Apparently, there was no security on duty and 4 Fiends managed to follow a Mercenary, barely able to call herself an adult, up to the top floor and fucking tortured and killed her." She gasped.

"Wait!" She spun back around as we moved to stand under the water, rinsing the soap from her skin. "Is that the hotel that you had me meet you at?" I nodded.

"It happened little more than a month ago and there still hasn't been any new information. I was going there to check the place myself, to see if maybe we missed something that was left behind. But then you fainted and everything else went out the window."

"I'm sorry," she said, like it was her fucking fault. I pressed my lips in annoyance. I hated how she thought she had to apologize for everything. Another fucking reason I wanted to tear Malachi apart.

"You apologize too much."

"I-" She stopped, realizing she was about to apologize again. I laughed as she shook her head. "Anyway," she continued, "So you think that Avery let them up there on purpose?" I could tell she got an idea in her head when her eyes lit up and she grabbed the washcloth from me. She started to do the same as I had, running it gently across my chest and arms. I enjoyed watching her touch me, her eyes scanning down my body as she went, though she ignored the area with my Spiral tattoo. I know that she was blaming herself for it, blaming herself for leaving and making me chase after her. But she didn't make me. She was entirely my reason for doing what I did, but it was exactly that. My choice.

"If she didn't, she at least knows who did." Her eyes shot back up to mine as her hand stopped just below my navel.

"Do you think it was Malachi?" I shrugged.

"I don't trust either of them. I already had my suspicions but then when Avery so easily admitted what she did that night just because he told her to, I realized that maybe she wasn't acting entirely of her own volition." She continued down her path, running the cloth down my legs as she avoided the area between them. Even as she did though, the thought of her being near it had it hardening again. Damn it. I was trying to behave because even though I should just be enjoying my wife today, I knew I was going to have to go to the club and remove any of the information I had on the Spider in case either of the Blackwoods came back. But if I kept getting a fucking hard on, it was going to make it really hard to leave.

She brought her hand back up, ready to stroke me with her wicked little hands and send me reeling. And it took all of my self-control to stop her from doing it. She looked up at me, her brow crinkled in confusion and dare I say anger.

"Do you not want me to?" Though she looked angry, there was a sadness in her tone. She stepped back, her arms dropping at her side like I had rejected her.

"Woah. Hey," I said, pulling her back to me. I lifted her off the ground, her legs instantly interlocking around my waist before I crushed her lips with mine. "I absolutely want you to."

"Then why stop me?" I realized then that she was pouting, a playful edge to her tone like she was taunting me. I sighed, relieved that she wasn't actually upset.

"Aren't you the one who said that I can't forget about work just because of sex?" She made a face, placing a finger on her chin like she was thinking.

"I don't remember saying that," she replied with a head shake. But her smile was cunning.

"Yeah?" I said as I placed her back on her feet before pushing her back against the wall. Her eyes went wide but her body melded against mine, her stiffened breasts pushing against my skin. "Perhaps I should remind you then." Slowly my mouth kissed down her chest as I moved downward, pulling one of her breasts into my mouth to swirl my tongue around her nipple.

"I may have said something like that," she cooed, the sarcasm in her tone on full display. "But I'm pretty sure I worded it differently." I tittered as I released her from my mouth before dropping to my knees in front of her. I hooked her thigh over my shoulder, placing not so gentle kisses along her skin before sliding my tongue along the length of her slick core. Her head leaned back, her eyes sliding shut as an unreserved, desperate cry escaped her. "We may have been discussing breakfast." She was trying so hard to keep up her playful little tone. But I silenced her next quip as I plunged my tongue inside of her again.

CHAPTER THIRTY-SEVEN

Arabella

I didn't think I'd be able to walk right for at least a week. That man fucked me so hard that it felt like he bruised my insides. Not that he promised anything less. But holy shit my legs felt like I had run a fucking marathon as I curled them under myself on the bed.

He said that he had to go back to the club to remove the files and information that he had on the Spider from his office in case Avery decided that she was going to return and take them by force. I didn't want to go on the off chance that she had been there when we got there. I wouldn't be able to look at her without feeling like she had taken a part of me when she told us the truth. The thought made me feel almost disgusted with myself. Because sure, the person that I was before was completely different than the one I was now. But I felt like Keiran should have been angrier than he was. He had every right to be because she took advantage of him that night. They may not have done anything and her being on top of him was just for show, but it still violated him in a way that made me want to claw her eyes out.

And that fact alone made me stay here, in the comfort of his bed. Our bed. And at some point, I had fallen asleep, the exhaustion of Keiran Stark's love overthrowing my scattered mind. I wasn't sure how long I had been out though before I awoke to a strange, muffled sob. I sat upright in a panic.

"Arabella." This time it wasn't muffled but there was something strange in the way Emery's voice slipped through the cracked door of the bedroom. I slipped on a pair of new leggings and a t-shirt before making my way back to the living room. As I cleared the hall, I stopped dead in my tracks.

Emery sat on the sofa, her brown eyes streaming with tears as Alexander sat beside her, his black hair, so much like Keiran's, falling in his darkened eyes as he ran his fingers through her hair. It was like he was trying to comfort her but the crooked smile that lifted his cruel face showed that it was only part of his game.

"Arabella, don't-"

"That's enough of the theatrics," he started, cutting Emery off as he slid his hand around her small throat. She stiffened and I took a step toward him, my Aura spilling out onto my fingertips. "One wrong move and I will snap her neck." His tone was deadly as he met my gaze. His black Aura spilled out around them, encircling Emery. My eyes settled on her, the bruises and cuts all over her skin finally drawing my attention before I shot my gaze back at him in anger.

"Stop hurting her," I snapped, taking another step toward them. I watched him tighten the energy around her, her whimper nearly shattering my self-control.

"That depends entirely on you, Arabella," he replied, his tone calm and collected. I took a step back, retracting my Aura and putting my hands up to show I wouldn't do anything. His Aura loosened slightly, though still swirled around her on high alert. "I knew you were powerful," he stated as my eyes settled on Emery's. I could see the fear in them, feel it spilling out of her. "I knew it the moment you threw your Aura for the first time, killing a Fiend like it was the easiest thing you'd ever done. I wasn't even able to do it right away. Even Keiran, who I am man enough to admit is more powerful than I am, had taken a while to learn something like that."

"What's your point?"

"This was why I kept you around for as long as I did; why I chose you to find the amulet," he continued, ignoring me. "So, imagine my surprise when the very thing I wanted had been within my reach the whole time, wearing cynicism like armor and hurling insults at me like a bratty teenager. It never even occurred to me that you could have also been the perfect vessel." I felt the breath leave my lungs. In a sick attempt at fixing his pride, Malachi revealed to the one man he hated more than anything, at least the one he had claimed to hate, the truth of my power. Gave away his weapon just so that he could have the upper hand.

"I'm assuming you sent Avery to the club so that Keiran would investigate, and I'd be left alone." He laughed, a cruel and manipulative sound.

"You always were more intelligent than most," he taunted. He twisted the wrist that wasn't wrapped around Emery to look down at the watch he was wearing. "I'd say he and Taylor are about to have a run in at any moment now. Both can be quite temperamental. I wonder who will come out on top?" Emery whimpered again, her quiet sobs still echoing between us. "I got extra lucky when this one decided to follow Avery last night. She told me that she was one of Keiran's filthy little strays that he likes to collect." I winced at his words. I had called them his little band of strays too, but I never meant it in a negative way.

"Let her come to me and I'll go with you willingly." Emery's eyes dilated, the tears a constant stream as he used a tendril to slither across her mouth, silencing her sobs.

"Do I have your word?" he asks, the amusement on his face mocking me. I held up my hands again.

"I promise." He paused, like he was adding dramatic effect before letting go of Emery, his Aura dissipating enough for her to run to me. She slammed into me with a loud sob as I pulled her to my chest, wrapping my arms around her protectively. She hugged me tightly as I whispered into her ear. "As soon as I walk out of that door, call Keiran."

"Don't go, Arabella," she sobbed against me. "You can't go. I can't see you at all anymore once you walk out that door." I stare at her for a moment, the tension weighing heavy between us. I knew what she meant. As soon as I walked out of that door with this man, she had no idea what was going to happen because she couldn't see it. Whether that meant I was dead, or he was hiding me, I wasn't sure. I just knew that I couldn't let him touch her.

Ignoring the pleading on her face, I forcefully pushed her away from me to walk toward Alexander. He stood up, pleased with the outcome of this fucked up situation and reached for my arm. I side stepped it, moving toward the door.

"Don't fucking touch me."

"Always so feisty, Miss Blackwood. Oh wait," he laughed, pushing open the front door from behind me. "You're a Stark now. Welcome to the family, daughter in law." I heard an unhinged sob before the door slammed shut behind us.

CHAPTER THIRTY-EIGHT

Keiran

Something didn't feel right. My muscles were tense, the hair on the back of my neck stood with alarming force, and that little voice in my head was screaming at me that something was off. As I walked through the parking lot, in a hurry to get back to my bride after spending a large chunk of the day getting new locks and a security system for the club, I felt a heavy presence somewhere close by. I turned around, my eyes scanning the barely lit parking lot until they landed on a huge mass no more than 10 feet in front of me. He smiled at me, the movement unnatural as he took a step toward me.

"I've heard about you," he said, his voice booming as he moved more into the light. Huge was an understatement. There was no way this man was human. He stood taller than me by at least 6 inches and packed pounds of pure muscle on every inch of him. "He said that I should be worried about you." He was dressed in a dark green camo suit. A soldier simply following orders. But for who? "That I should be careful. You don't really seem that intimidating though." This time I grinned. It had been a while since I'd had a good fight.

"Now that hurts my feelings," I replied with wicked intent as I cracked my neck. "I put a lot of thought into my tough guy persona." I removed my suit jacket, tossing it onto the hood of a car close by as I unbuttoned my cuff links to roll up my sleeves to my elbows. He chuckled, a deep boisterous sound.

"You really are his son." I tensed up at those words.

"Alexander sent you." It wasn't a question, but he nodded anyway, a gleam in his eye like he was proud of that fact.

"Told me to distract you long enough for him to find the girl." My Aura spilled out of me at an alarming pace, and he laughed again at my reaction. "I gotta be honest. I underestimated her as well. After I broke her ribs, I didn't think she'd be able to bounce back so quickly. Maybe I should heed his warning and keep my guard up around you." I was trying to keep my anger at bay, keep myself from taking his life too quickly. I was going to enjoy hurting him the way he hurt Arabella.

"You did that?" I kept my voice calm as he nodded with joy. "Gotta say bud. I've been dying to repay the favor." I took a step closer to him, the distance between us less than the size of a car at this point. I watched his excessive muscles tense though he tried to hide it with another laugh.

"Should you succeed," he said, his body shifting into a ready stance. "I'm aware that I would deserve it." He lunged for me, closing that small space within seconds. I side stepped him, barely dodging his massive fist flying toward my face. He flipped back around, launching another punch toward me that I narrowly avoided.

"For someone so large you are quite agile," I taunted before jumping back to avoid his heavy foot coming up for a roundhouse kick. "Although if you keep using up so much of your energy, this is going to be over too quickly. I wanted to enjoy killing you." He lunged at me again, his large fingers snaking their way around my throat. But as they started to tighten, I reached up and hit him square in the jaw with an uppercut infused with a small fraction of my Aura. It was a move that Arabella had taught me once when she was trying to spar with me. She still lost, the annoyance on her face by that fact still making me laugh. He let go of me as he staggered back, blood seeping from the corner of his lips.

"You made me bite my tongue." His voice was shocked like he didn't think I'd be able to hit him. I was grinning as I positioned myself for another attack and just as I thought he would, he lunged at me again.

"Are you just going to use brute strength?" I dodged him again, at this point doing more of a dance than actually fighting him. "Why not use your Aura?" I watched something cross in his face, a deep hidden pain that he wanted to suppress. "Are you human?" He came for me again, my jaw aching in heavy protest as his fist made contact this time. "And here I thought we were starting to make progress." I gripped my dislocated chin, groaning as I popped it back into place.

"Shut the fuck up," he snapped, taking a step back. "I'm not human." There was a trepidation in his voice, his arrogance faltering for a fraction of a second. He straightened up again, his large foot coming back at me from the front, probably in the same way that he had kicked Arabella to break her ribs. The thought pissed me off as I grabbed his foot and held it for a second before pushing it back at him with force. He stumbled backward. If he only wanted to use force, then so be it. He may have been bigger than me, but I still knew how to throw my own strength around when needed. "I'm not human," he muttered again, and by his staggered breathing I knew that he really had been using all his energy in the hopes of taking me down quickly.

"So, you've said," I replied. We continued like this for what felt like several minutes but was probably only seconds. One would throw a punch and the other would dodge or take the hit before repeating the cycle. I watched his stamina draining though which still made me wonder why he wouldn't just try using his Aura to save some of that energy. "Would you like a rest?" My tone was taunting as he leaned forward on his knees, heavy breaths gasping from his lungs. He tried swinging again but missed dramatically. "I might have a water bottle in my car if you need it."

"He fucking took it," he yelled like he was answering an unspoken question. He dropped to his knees, a sorrowful look on his face that almost made me feel bad for the guy. "I wanted nothing to do with him, so he fucking took it."

"Took what?" I was no longer taunting him, my tone serious as I stood in front of him.

"My Aura." His voice had dropped, the sounds of the city around us nearly drowning it out. "He took it because I told him I didn't want to be his lackey. He killed them all and then he fucking took it." Tears were now streaming down his pained face as he sat back on his heels, dropping his head in his hands. Something about seeing a man as strong as he was so completely broken was sobering.

"Then why continue to do so?"

"Because I have nothing left." I knew that feeling of defeat, of complete and utter despair. "I deserve nothing. But I am going to ask you anyway as a man, moments from his death." Finally, he looked back up at me, conviction on his face. "I will be happy to die by your hand, Keiran. To die by the hands of a man that truly fights for what he wants is a death that so few of us get to have. I only ask that you take the head of Alexander Stark with even just a small thought of me in your mind when you do it." I stared at him, my face holding a hidden expression as I sucked on my teeth. I stepped toward him, gripping his large, hardened jaw in my hand to force him to look into my eyes.

"What's your name?"

"It doesn't matter," he muttered.

"It does," I replied. "If I'm to take your life, I'd like to know your name." As I spoke, my Aura spilled from my fingers, dancing across his skin as it wrapped around his neck. His eyes went wide as it started to tighten slowly.

"Taylor," he breathed harshly. I stared into his large dark eyes as I sat with his words and watched with an amused expression as I cut off his breathing. He didn't struggle. Didn't move to break away and continue to fight for the man that had taken everything from him. He sat there and accepted that this was going to be the way he died.

I pulled my Aura back into me, his gasps for air sputtering between us. He fell forward onto his hands, coughing into the dirty ground. When he caught his breath, he turned his head up to look at me.

"B- why?" I squatted down in front of him, his head still twisted up toward me as he bowed on the ground. My voice was harsh.

"Because I know that the worst way to punish a man that wants to die, is to keep him alive." His eyes went wide. Taylor opened his mouth to speak but snapped it shut when a loud shriek pierced our ears and I turned to see Emery barreling towards us as she cried. She slammed into me, throwing her little arms around my neck as I embraced her. "What's wrong?"

"I can't see her," she sobbed. "I can't tell where she is." Panic flooded through me.

"Emery what do you mean?"

"He knows, Keiran," she yelled, out of breath from a mix of running and crying. "He fucking knows about her, and he took her!" I bent down and grabbed Taylor by the neck.

"You're gonna tell me everything starting with who the

fuck told Alexander about Arabella's power!"

CHAPTER THIRTY-NINE

Taylor slouched in the chair he was tied to, the blood starting to dry on his nose and mouth as he teetered between awake and unconscious. He was more than willing to talk. I just needed something to take the anger out and the man that broke my wife's ribs was a great way to do that. Though I had felt sorry for him for what Alexander had done, it still didn't mean I was going to let him off the hook. He was going to make up for all of the shitty things he did while under Alexander's employment starting with me breaking every bone in his body that I could without killing him.

Though, the person I really wanted on the receiving end of this aggression was Malachi. The fucking snake went to the one man that he fucking hated more than himself just because he didn't get what he wanted. I had people scouring Hallowed Haven to look for him but the fucker seems to have disappeared.

"Hey boss." I snapped around, my nerves on edge as I grabbed Liam by the throat instinctively and squeezed. He started coughing, clawing at my hands as his soft green eyes went wide. I let go, dropping him back down to the ground.

"Sorry," I muttered. "I'm getting antsy."

"I know," his voice was strained, his windpipe fucked up from me grabbing him. "I was trying to let you know that someone was here to see you." I pushed past him, leaving him in my office with Taylor's beaten-up body as I made my way out to the main floor of the club. I had decided to close it down for the day this morning so that I could heighten the security. Thankfully I did because if I had been surrounded by people right now, there would have been a massacre.

My eyes scanned the room until they landed on a crying Jezebel. She sat at the bar, her cries echoing through the empty building. As if she felt my presence, she looked up, her sorrowful eyes meeting mine on another sob. I cleared the room, my face unreadable as I approached her.

"So, it's true?" she asked, her tone breaking at the end. "He knows?" I nodded. "Oh Keiran." She hugged me but I couldn't return the gesture. She looked at me puzzled. "You don't think I had something to do with this do you?" I lifted a brow.

"Do you?" She started crying again, shaking her head violently.

"Regardless of whether or not she came from me, she was still my daughter," she said. "I promised Elizabeth on her death bed that I would protect that girl until I couldn't anymore. I never would have told Alexander the truth about where she came from. Malachi and Avery acted on their own." Her face had grown angry as she swiped at her tears. "That's why I'm here. I found this." She reached behind her to grab a stack of papers from the bar counter and handed them to me. They looked like bank statements over the last year, starting from the moment I took Malachi's place as Proctor and replaced all his compromised members with those that weren't fiercely loyal to him.

Every single month, on the dot, there were 2 despots from the same account number. 2 very large deposits. But for what?

"You had no idea?" I asked. "Millions of dollars were being put in your bank account and you never questioned it?"

"Malachi had said that it was because the hotel garnered high rollers. That they didn't like to be known because they were high ranked members of society, so they did it anonymously while they stayed there. You have to believe me, Keiran. I knew nothing about it." I wanted to but I was finding it hard to trust anyone's word at this point. I sighed, closing my eyes as I rubbed my temples with my fingers. "I want to find her just as much as you do." My eyes snapped open, shooting her a look that made her shut up.

"I doubt that," I snapped. "None of you lifted a fucking finger to bring her back in the last 5 years. What makes now any different?" I knew my words were too harsh, but I was angry as I stormed away from her, needing some fresh air. As the breeze hit my face the moment I stepped outside, the first cold weather of the autumn season enveloping me like she was trying to soothe my aching heart, I inhaled deeply. I slid my eyes shut, trying to keep my mind from thinking of what Alexander was doing to her.

I knew that he wouldn't kill her. If he did, there goes that power that he was desperately seeking. He needed her alive, at least until he found a way to transfer it to himself. If that was what he really wanted. And how did I know if he hadn't already figured out a way to do it?

"Motherfucker," I yelled, punching the wall beside me so hard my knuckles split.

"You always did have such a short temper." I flipped around at his voice. He stood there, a devil mask covering his face as the Spider stood a few feet in front of me. His hands, which were covered in scars that were barely visible in the light of the dawning morning, hung out in front of him in mock surrender. "Especially when it came to Alexander." Why was that voice so familiar?

"What do you want?" He moved his right hand toward his face, the quick gesture pulling my Aura around me swiftly in defense. He laughed, a hallow sound spilling from behind the mask as he shook his head. He gripped the bottom of it, the intricate design made of glass, and with the quickness of a snail started lifting it off his face.

"Not only have the Blackwoods betrayed you," he said, his fingers stilling just before revealing who he was. "But they also betrayed me as well." With very limited hesitation, he lifted the mask the rest of the way, shaking his shaggy blond hair down around his face as his eyes met mine. Our mother's fucking eyes. For the first time in my life, my legs trembled.

"That's not fucking possible," I muttered, my eyes going wide. He smiled, the scar on his face from a hunt when we were younger, crinkling around his left eye.

"Hello little brother," Damian said. "I think it's time we finally have a little chat."

EPILOGUE

Arabella

The room was dark, the mildew scent of the wet stone walls the only thing giving me an inkling of my surroundings. Someone was in the room with me though, I could feel them watching me as I struggled with the chains holding me to the ceiling. His cruel laugh filtered through my ears from behind me.

"I used to think that you would never retain a thing that I taught you." Malachi's voice was like nails on a chalkboard. "But you put up one hell of a fight when I tried to get you down here." I could feel him as he moved to stand in front of me. I couldn't see but I spat at him and I knew it hit. He stumbled back, a sound of disgust leaving his lips before I felt his hand across my face with such force I tasted blood in my mouth. "You fucking bitch." He moved closer, gripping the back of my head as he yanked my neck back and his hot breath spilled across my face. "I can't wait to fucking break you." The room suddenly filled with a dull light as a heavy door at the top of a set of stairs that I could now see, opened. It illuminated Malachi's cruel face, his lips pulled back in a twisted snarl and his eyes wild with a fury I had never seen before.

"All in due time, Malachi," Alexander's voice seeped into the room as he descended the stairs, and walked with an arrogance around him like he had already won in his eyes. He stopped behind Malachi, waving a hand to dismiss him as he stepped out of his way. The action made me laugh.

"What's so funny," Malachi spat. I smiled, the blood from his slap spilling from my mouth to slide down my chin.

"It must eat you alive to know you'll always be second to one of them." I couldn't move my arms so I nudged my head toward Alexander. "A Stark will always be your better in every way." He raised his hand like he was going to hit me again but Alexander stopped it.

"Leave us," he said and I watched with a twisted sense of enjoyment as he hesitated to do what he said. "Now." With his head dropping in defeat he turned from us, walking up the stairs in a delicious walk of shame. "I must say that it makes me quite happy that you've embraced your spot in this family." My eyes snapped to Alexander's. "The name Stark truly does look good on you."

"Is this my wedding gift from you? Your blessing?" I spit blood at his feet. "You can fucking keep it." He laughed, the sound echoing around us. His hand shot out and gripped my chin hard to tilt my head up toward his face. I pulled away as hard as I could, the reaction probably already leaving a bruise on my skin.

"Good. Keep that fight in you, Arabella. You're going to need it."

"Are you going to kill me?" It wasn't a question out of desperation. Purely out of curiosity. I hadn't realized he had kept one hand behind his back the whole time, concealing the syringe that was now being stabbed into my neck until it was too late. The poison shot through me, the rotten smell of the belladonna filling my nose as he turned away from me.

"No," he said as my vision started to blur. "But you are going to wish that I would." That arrogant fucking laugh and the fading sound of his foot steps was the last thing I remembered before my head slumped forward and the poison overtook me.

ABOUT THE AUTHOR

Hannah Crawford

Spawned from the depths of the Underworld (Riverside, California), Hannah Crawford spends most of her days trying to broker a deal with the Fae that cursed her family for stealing their archives. She finds herself settled in Colorado with her husband, close family, and an army of cats to help fend off the Supernatural folk. When she's not wishing that the apocalypse would start, she's usually hiding in a dark corner with a book and some coffee or crying over an anime character that deserved better.